VITA

Dream Big!

Vita Cook

Hearing Colors

The Birth of Anniston

outskirtspress
DENVER, COLORADO

Hearing Colors
The Birth of Anniston
All Rights Reserved.
Copyright © 2014 Vita Coop
v2.0

Cover Image by Shannon Butler

Outskirts Press, Inc.
http://www.outskirtspress.com

ISBN: 978-1-4787-4244-9

Outskirts Press and the "OP" logo are trademarks belonging to Outskirts Press, Inc.

PRINTED IN THE UNITED STATES OF AMERICA

For

Superman

Acknowledgements

I possess a lingering gratitude to my creative team and sounding board. Without you, I could not have done this. Words can't express the gratitude I feel toward my twin sister, Shekita. I was born with a best friend and it just doesn't get any better than that. To Author, Monique Nixon, my editor and professional constructive criticizer, I am grateful for your gift. Writers, Kenyetta Easley, Akeci Gremond, and Flenardo, all lovers of words, helped me through this project when you didn't even know it. You had no idea I was writing a book when I would vent to you about struggles as a creative mind. Your personal adventures with words pushed me more to complete this journey. Kinua Bradford and Melita Heard, you have listened to my ideas and supported me in absolutely everything that I have ever done. Shannon Butler of S'own Designs, my cover designer, a book is naked without a cover. My body of work needed clothing and you designed it. Thank you all for the creativity.

Many thanks to my publishing and production team at OP: My Title Production Supervisor, RebeccaA, Production Manager, WendyS and a very special thanks to my Author Rep, Jamie Belt for holding my hand during this entire process.

I act in appreciation of my mom, Sara, my grandmother, Irene and all of my great Aunts for making me strong. Special thanks to my brother, Darius, and my children, Asia and Donovan. Jordan, Nadia, Sanaa and Kingdyn, Tee Tee loves you. To my Uncles and Aunt, Frank, Byron and Brenda, I thank you all dearly. To my Alabama, Illinois, Michigan and New Jersey family, it takes a village and I'm grateful to have you all as my village.

To my advisers and dear friends, Krystal Sears and Erika van Putten, there are no words!

My sisterhood: My 95' home team, My Cobb Family, Nicole, Maletha, and a special thanks to Sylvia for allowing me to timely finish this project by saving the laptop's life. Ladies, if walls could talk!

My brotherhood: Montrael B, D Russell, Dashawn, Michael B, Hugh, Eric, Phillip, Chip, Jamal and Jawa; somebody should break down the walls so they can't talk!

A very deserving thank you to my Aunt Louise for giving me my first book and my deepest gratitude goes to Richard Mckenzie and Terry Miller who died believing in me.

Chapter 1

*I*ce cream, big'ole spoon... My shopping list is complete. Clearly I have no appetite for things that are good for me as I have indulged in several rendezvous' with a married man and gone for multiple helpings. Comfort food has come to cradle me like a blanket during this time of guilt. The market will be my next stop after this doctor's appointment. Only in my life is my soul mate married. The one I love is loved by someone else. That someone doesn't know that he meets me... that he watches me when I sleep... that his heart rate increases when he touches me. This someone does not excite him as I do. Therefore, she will never understand the passion, the reason for such betrayal. But, I shall come to recognize her request. I will inform her of our affair. Though I never meant to hurt her, this pain will grow like a toddler. Maybe she should add ice cream to her shopping list as well. She will need to feed the pain. I often thought of what I would say if confronted. It's fruition time. I need to do this now as it's still my first trimester and I can conceal the pregnancy. I feel as if I should be standing in a cold room with strangers admitting to my addiction. Hi, my name is Anni and I'm addicted to a married man. Anni Townsend, the other woman.

How Baby and I came to be...

"I designed that." I take so much pleasure in uttering that simple phrase. It's time for my alumni event and I was asked to help plan and design. It makes my heart happy to be a part of this. Let the good times roll. It's the day of and I've seen so many beautiful, familiar faces. The food arrives and those familiar faces spark with satisfaction. It's a hit! Walking off to mingle, I am full of contentment as I see more familiar faces from my past. All are dressed in alumni paraphernalia. My face hurts from smiling and laughing. It's time to put some effort into going to the after party. The club in my hometown is a breeding ground for women, born and bred, to catch a man with a "good job". Morals don't seem to matter. It's hilarious to watch so I expect my face to hurt a little more. Laughter is on its way. I'm happy to see more old friends gliding through the space; feeling no pain as the alcohol has numbed them. Then, I hear a voice in my ear, a sexy voice that utters, "Hey gorgeous". I turn to see the face that matches this voice. My eyes meet his and it was just who I thought. Heart races... Smile hardens on my face. This is a different kind of happy. He hugs me and now my body is beaming. My awareness of him heightens. All others fall victim to the background. My perception is missing. He stands still with a glow around him. There is no noise. He has robbed me of my senses. I'm hearing colors...

I snapped out of it as we said our goodbyes. My brother Alec glided me across the dance floor before people noticed that I was stuck in some sort of celestial perception of this man. I'm glad Alec was with me. He was a godsend. Being a twin was like having a human synonym. As Alec drove to our favorite after hours spot, I couldn't stop thinking about Baby. I had not seen him in a long time. We existed only through text messages and an occasional email. My mind goes back to the night he slept next to me. That night my brother came over to my place to spend the weekend. He brought Pre-judge Baby with him...

I saw Baby, my abdomen clenched and my brain determined he was the only one in the room. I was experiencing my first phantasm of his electric blue eyes; later I would describe to my friends as a visual orgasm. A black man with blue eyes... His long locks of hair begged me to grab them. I obeyed. Before I knew it, I was twirling his hair and hopelessly gazing in his eyes.

"A hand shake would have sufficed," he says smiling.

I reply, "I apologize. But, your eyes are intense enough to give an aspirin a headache".

"Alec, you were right. She makes one hell of a first impression. Hi, Anacelia. I'm Zieg. Family calls me Baby. I've heard so much about you."

"Likewise, I'm pleased to finally meet my brother's literal partner in crime. What do you two lawyers have planned for fun tonight?"

"You'll just have to see little sister. But first we have to pick up Celeste."

Celeste was Alec's girlfriend of many years. Being my twin's girlfriend, she had accomplished being the closest thing to a female best friend I've ever had. We went to the cafe where my friend Jax was the saxophonist. Celeste was in the backseat with me so we could whisper. We parked and Baby got out and opened my car door and escorted me. It was very chivalrous. I was so taken by him that I stepped out of my shoe and stumbled backward into the parking space next to us. *Headlights came out of nowhere and a car almost hit me. Baby grabs me by the waist and pulls me to him to keep the car from hitting me; part two of the chivalry.*

That night of spoken word and live music lead Baby and I into a long discussion of awareness. We shared so many things and so many interests. He took my breath away. We were intertwined, a double helix of common interests. What I craved, he possessed. I wanted him. My mind insisted that my body stop for a moment so they could converse and figure out how to accept this new strain of pleasure. It doesn't make sense. I just met him.

He interrupts my thoughts. "Anni, I would like to rest with you. I will not try anything my dear. I just want to see how it feels to wake up next to you."

In agreement, we go back to my place.

The walk through my dark, quiet, house spoke volumes. We're at the foot of my bed and his eyes ask the question: Shall we?

"Yes. You may sleep here." I answer welcomingly.

"Thanks gorgeous."

This would be the first time he calls me gorgeous.

I rest partially wrapped in sheets and in his arms. His arms should be my permanent address. The window is open. A cool, wet mist from the rain blows in and deposits on my face. His voice echoed into my ear like a speaker. I was in a 3D movie... ...

"Anni! Snap out of it. We're here. Let's eat."

Alec interrupted my daydreaming of the night I met Baby. Alec and I sat and talked about the alumni event we just left as well as discussing his proposal to Celeste. I add that Baby should have been my husband."

"Anni, you only spent one night with him. You weren't even intimate. How can you say he should have married you?"

Alec's phone rings. It's Baby! Alec removes himself from the table, but I can still hear him.

"Well, you can tell her yourself." He gives the phone to me while shaking his head as if in disbelief. I take the phone and pull a "hello" from the bedrock of my soul.

"Anni, this may sound extreme but I feel you are the person that I am meant to be with."

"Baby, I was just telling Alec the same of you."

"Gorgeous, I don't know why I'm telling you this now. Maybe your presence tonight has fueled my words. I know my timing is terrible."

"Baby, I'm glad you've finally shared your feelings as it has opened up a new line of communication for us."

"Anni take care." He sounds so final. As if he was saying goodbye forever. But, I reciprocate with a warmer salutation.

"Goodnight Baby."

Giving Alec's phone back, I bask in the words I have just heard. Alec reveals a surprise as well. "I can't believe he told me he should have married you instead."

"INSTEAD?"

"Yes, Anni. Didn't you know? He's married."

"No, I didn't know."

I can find no words.

I manage a couple of bites before I ask if we can leave. "I want to get some sleep."

"Yes, sis. I'm sorry."

The morning comes fast. My feet, hitting the floor, trigger the episodes from last night. My thoughts are locked on Baby. He's married, (Shaking my head). I'm experiencing some unfamiliar and unwelcomed feelings. I don't think I can eat breakfast. Back to bed I go. I can't sleep. I replay the filtered telephone convo from last night over and over. No wonder he was so final. He just wanted me to know how he felt. I reach out to him via email...

Baby,

You're an absolute doll. You take my breath whenever I see you. I just learned that you're married. Apparently, I've been living under a rock. But then again, I often disassociated myself from any discussion involving you due to my feelings showing. It was safer that way. However, congratulations on your journey.

The one that got away,

Anni

HE REPLIES....

Gorgeous,

I can't stop thinking about you. I never meant to derail you. I thought you knew of my marriage. It was an arrangement orchestrated by my parents. We had a huge wedding for election purposes. It was a major spectator event. So, I thought you were aware. I always wondered how you felt about it. Alec and Celeste were arranged and they fell madly for each other, but I can't say the same. I was thinking of you when I took those vows. That night we spent together was amazing. You are my prototype and I need you around me. I came back to life when I saw you. I just can't see my life without you. You are what's missing. I've been living vicariously through the remarks of Alec. Please contact me so that I can live through you. Just so that I may have the hand on experience that I've been craving.

The one that chases you,

Baby

I've read this email a thousand times. I'm going to have to deal with him sooner or later... Possibly sooner... Alec and Celeste are having a party. I'm sure Baby will attend. What should I do? Alec will be heartbroken if I'm not there.

One week has passed since the email and I've thought only of Baby. However, I must get ready for the party so that I don't disappoint my brother with my absence. Fedan (Fey) will be there as well. Fey was our friend from college. We had even settled into the same job. She had gotten really close to my family as her relatives weren't really the family type. Smart but always saw a mirage when it came to love.

She married this asshole, Joseph, who seemed great at first. He showered her with the thought of love. She went on and on about Joe King until he popped the question at a waffle house in the middle of the night. *Charming...* This below average Joe always wanted to be more than what he was. Joe was the result of fruitlessness working on a weak mind. He never wanted to put in the work. She actually married Joe King. Celeste and I called him "Joking" because he was a joke---a coward hiding behind things he couldn't afford. However, we also saw Fey as a fake at times and called her "Faking". Fey King always says she is okay when she is not. She tells us this so we won't worry. She is actually just loyal. The connective tissue disorder she had been diagnosed with has made her submit more to this grown boy. One Mother's day he choked her and broke her nose, in her dream house. He was a vivid liar. She stuck with him after the diagnosis. He blamed the incident on drinking and stress. One bankruptcy and a marriage counselor later, they are still together. He won't come to the party. He never supports her and he does not like any of us.

I sit down at my beautifully mirrored vanity to get ready for this party. I don't know this woman in front of me. I recognize the long, wavy hair and caramel skin, but her brown eyes seem different. Her smile hasn't been present in a week. Funny, she looks so shattered in this perfect mirror. The little black dress hanging behind her will be grateful for the 5 pounds lost from her vanishing appetite. (Sighing) I look at the mirror and say aloud "Anni, *pour yourself a drink, put on some lipstick and get yourself together*". My inner Elizabeth Taylor speaks while my tresses channel a young Diana Ross.

I glide on my dress and my favorite red peep toes. I stand a petite 5'4" with heels on. Baby once told me I had the heart and soul of a 6'4" man. My mother had blessed me with trajectory curves, a 36-26-40 build. I'm a brick house with a garage! No necklace or nail polish tonight. I planned only diamond earrings and red lips to match my shoes. Time to rock and roll! Alec sends a car for me. I get in and Celeste and Fey are waiting with opened arms. A girl's night will do me some good.

We arrive and Alec's place is decorated very tastefully. The hors d oeuvres are enchanting and the pastries were mind blowing. I parade around to find a server in this sea of all black; Celeste's idea to have an all-black attire party. I need a drink. I find my favorite Moscato and hear the words "I'm sure those red shoes with legs attached belong to Anacelia." I can no longer walk and turning around is impossible. Once again I recognize the voice so I keep moving, proceeding to the outside of the house. I gulp the glass of Moscato and eat the strawberry garnish. The wind blows the smell of chocolate and I know he's standing behind me. It's the same smell from years ago. He wraps his arms around my shoulders and smells my hair.

"Anni, you smell just like I remember... the same as that night. I've never kissed you. I need to know what it's like."

I turned around and offered him the back of my hand. He grinned but accepted my invitation. He kissed the back of my hand and takes my empty glass inside to replace it with another.

"Don't move," He utters.

I moved. I scurried around the house and said my goodbyes to my friends and to my brother.

"I have to go." I muttered aloud.

They all understand and offer to walk me to the car. Declining their offers, I issued hugs. The walk down the driveway seemed like the longest walk I had ever hiked. The butterflies in my stomach accompany me. Even a kiss on the hand from this man proves to be quite memorable.

Damn, he's waiting at the car. "Anni, don't leave because of me. I'll go."

"Baby, I have already said goodbye to everyone."

"Gorgeous?" He requests a kiss.

Before I could answer, he steps into my space and stirs up those butterflies. He held me for minutes with no words. My arms are at my side. I can't bring myself to touch him. This is the same embrace that intoxicated me before. He continues to hold me and kisses my cheek. His arms release and he places his hands softly on my neck, thumbs outlining the kisses he just left on my cheek.

I look up and his eyes kidnap mine. His nose and my nose touch. I can feel his breath on my lips. He is so close that his eyelashes are brushing my skin. We were exchanging breaths. A person's mouth should not water when thinking of another person. What was happening? Imperfect describes my wanting. Perfection describes my need. When I'm near him, I feel the need to escape. My brain and heart are at war. My middle seems to want to be the peacemaker. My middle wants to give in, sending a message to my heart and my mind; a peace treaty to be signed by guilt. I wanted him to kiss me badly.

"Anacelia, please say that I may kiss you."

"Yes, you may."

A kiss should not be a decision... A formation should not have to occur; mimicking clouds before a storm. Uncertainty clouds my brain, mirroring the storm. Indecisiveness comes like rain. Rain, rain, go away. I sigh with caution. It's dangerous to think these thoughts. I'm careful not to wake my other insecurities during this storm. My heart pounds like thunder. The urges come like lightning. I'm holding my head down to keep from getting drenched with the indecisiveness... Do I? Don't I? The storm is building...brewing... I lift my head and it's over... I go into the storm... Eyes fluttering like a bird after the storm... My thoughts are no longer cloudy. *I can see clearly now for the rain has gone...* The indecisiveness has gone. My lips part like the sea... and land just where I want... It's amazing how something you can't see can be so colorful… as that of a rainbow… I had to go through a storm to get my rainbow…

His lips touch mine. He buries his head into my shoulders and says, "Finally, I've waited so long". He delivers another kiss to my neck and I stop him. I feel faint stepping toward the car. He opens the car door for me to get in and says, "thank you."

I get in the car and he leaves me thinking, "did he just thank me for kissing him?" The pleasure was mine.

My thoughts are invading me and riding in this car has me all bottled up. I've been lately considering myself to be a message in a bottle, awaiting discovery to free my thoughts to a chosen recipient. I think I have chosen the one. Nothing else could prove to be so care-free. Sharing, declaring, and reading someone's thoughts carry such a message within itself. My message; without him I wouldn't have known the power of listening, the art of focusing and the freedom of a kiss on the neck. Love, art, power, and freedom exhibit a life well lived and more to conquer. Without him I wouldn't have developed a keen awareness of touch… a touch that produces my smiles… An awareness of smell, the sense most linked to memory. Any memory of him is a gift to me.

An annoying beep is coming from my clutch. My text message notification is going off and I'm sure it's a message from Baby.

It reads. "I'm smiling beyond what I'm used to. I don't know how to explain it."

I respond, "Don't explain… Just describe it and it will come easy to you. Describe what you feel. What do you feel, Baby?"

"I feel you. Like an amputee who reaches for his limb that's no longer there. Have your driver take you to my corporate condo. I will send you the address."

Oh my. I have no idea what response to send. I'm so curious. Without another thought, I respond, "yes".

Driving miles to see him… That damned kiss! It was a gateway drug. I am in danger of becoming addicted, but I must know where the high will take me. I chase the high down 285. Cars are speeding past on the expressway but they aren't racing nearly as fast as my heart. The rush! My seatbelt can't contain all of this spontaneous energy. I'm sitting on the edge of the seat. I've made several attempts to relax my legs but they tighten more at each mile marker that brings me closer to this man. The car slows in speed and stops but my internal motor is still running. Only he can pacify this curiosity. I walk in and his eyes intensely calm me. He's a walking oxymoron. He says to me, "I've been so worried about you. Please tell me what you're feeling. He strokes my hair. "Let it go. Open the cage and just let it fly out." He trails his fingers from the side of my face down to my chin. He props my mouth open with his thumb and kisses me lightly. I want to talk to him but I can't. I want to hear his voice tell me it's going to be okay. He realizes I'm not going to tell him my thoughts and he hushes my lips with his finger as he now wants to have a silent conversation. A conversation of touch only...

I hunger to hear his voice. I want his voice to be here, in my ear. His kisses are having conversations with my cheek, with my neck, with my abdomen, with my... my... my... No words... It's near. It's such an emotional conversation. I'm feeling it, tears are coming but not from my eyes, now, he has no words. My emotion has his tongue...

I need to get to know him better so I introduce myself. My fingers crawl underneath his shirt and underneath the rim of his boxers; flirting with his button, getting to know his zipper. Then, I reach in for the handshake. A firm handshake... This introduction was magnifying. Intensity heightens the touch of my fingers. My mind processes that this is where I'm comfortable. I hold him and my body reacts. My mind and body are giving out orders. I get a chill but my body heats up at the same time. My body is reacting as if it's fighting itself, a viral romance, a sexual flu... My temperature turns up and my body sneezes from the waist down. All this just from touching him... Then what's to come? He is the illness and the antidote. I succumb to the strain.

I wake up in the bed alone, looking at one red heel by the door. I can't imagine where the mate could be. Has he left the house? I turn to see a note on a napkin with a platter of Hazelnut spread, toast and fruit. The note reads...

Anni,

"You're missing an earring. It somehow got lost in the oblivion. Look under your pillow."

Grasping at my ears I drop the napkin note and reach under the pillow. I'm staring at a blue Tiffany box. I'm captivated. Inside is the most stunning pair of princess cut earrings trimmed with baguettes. I don't even notice that he is now standing next to me...

"Baby, when did you do this?"

"I sent for them, Anni..."

I can't accept them, as I shook my head in disbelief.

"Please just consider them a replacement." He begged.

"Baby, we could have just looked for the other one."

"Anni, we can't even find your other shoe!"

I smile. "Touche..."

"May I place them for you?"

"Yes, Baby."

Have I ever even said no to this man?

I walk over to the mirror, 1800 thread count sheet wrapping my curves like a designer gown. "They are beautiful. You've taken me by such surprise. I need to absorb all of this."

He stands behind me holding me, admiring me as well as the new gift he has placed in my ears. He pulls my head back softly to admire them and my neck at the same time. He kisses my neck and I melt.

"Anni, it's ok. Allow me to comfort you."

"Baby, I have to go. I have a brunch with Fey to discuss an event. I must get dressed and leave."

"Will you notify me when you're done? We should discuss some things."

"I imagine so. I need to get dressed and find my clothes in this beautiful concrete jungle of a house."

"Look in the bathroom, Anni."

"Oh great, you already found my clothes!"

As I walk into the bathroom, there is a red box labeled "Macy's." OMG, this damn man has also replaced my shoes! How? I also find undergarments, jeans and a beautiful sheath. I don't know if I should be excited or confused. He clearly sent for these items as well.

"Baby, How? When?"

"Anni, it was no problem. I didn't want you to be late. But, tell Fey I said thanks when you meet."

"She was in on this?" He gifts my forehead with a kiss... another kiss to my nose... another kiss to my mouth and another surprises me below my waist." He slips my new shoes on for me but spreads my legs apart. My entire thinking process has been suppressed. I have completely shut down as he rubs the inside of my thighs... I'm going to be late...

Chapter 2

How am I supposed to function? I can't possibly make it through this meeting with Fey. However, I couldn't wait to discuss Baby's antics. I am mesmerized by this man. October is closing out. Zombies and vampires are everywhere and the only thing haunting me is his absence. Festivities are widespread but the fear of not seeing him is even bigger. My judgment wears a mask like that of the masqueraders parading around... It's a perfect Holiday for a secret romance. With sealed identities, our first kiss could have been published out in the open without the chaotic inquisitive stares from others. Trying to put this thought to rest, I sit for dinner not hungry because I just swallowed a hard pill of confusion. That damned kiss was like a switch. How do I turn it off? I can't. I can't turn it off.

I notice the delight Fey has taken in my situation. She's getting a kick out of this.

"Fey, you are enjoying this way too much."

"Anni, Let me live vicariously through you. I'm going through hell with Joe. My sister called and notified me of a foreclosure notice in the paper. We're losing the house. Joe has missed several mortgage payments and hid it from me. Since he works nights, he's at home during the day and intercepts the mail. I had no idea! Apparently, that's not the only thing he's doing at night."

"What do you mean, Fey?"

"He's cheating. I got an email from a woman."

"Fey, I'm so sorry. I'm going on and on about my secret little union with Baby. This must be a slap in the face."

"Anni, we all know Baby's marriage is a fake. My husband is just a selfish bastard. He only cares about himself and he will get what he deserves. Baby would never try to hurt his wife, even if she is just a trophy. He's not that kind of person. He just fell madly for you and he is dealing with it now."

"I suppose. It's still wrong. But, what kind of future can I have with a man who marries for a show?"

"A future that's brighter than marrying for comfort as I did. My marriage is a joke!

What do ya know...? (APPEARS JOE KING)... "Speak of the Devil and he appears."

"How are you Ms. Celie?" Joe asks nonchalantly.

Everybody else calls me Anni. He is the only person who shortens my name, Anacelia, to Celie, a character from *The Color Purple*. He thinks he is hilarious. I find no pain in it due to *The Color Purple* being my favorite movie. The jokes on him... I just reply, "Hey Mister," with a "touché" smirk. He's reminiscent of the character as he is control-ling and violent. He tried to beat the hell out of Fey on Mother's Day but Fey is strong. He even ripped all of the clothes in her suitcase before one of our girl's trips. Bastard!

Poor Fey... She always tries to keep the peace because she helps raise his daughter, Kerrigan, from another relationship. Fey is all she has.

Fey interrogates him. "Joe, Why are you here so early? Where have you been? "

Joe answers, "I got a bite to eat from Chick-fil-A and rushed right back here.

"Joe, Chick-fil-A isn't open on Sunday."

Laughter blurts right out of my mouth and I lean back in my chair wishing I had popcorn to see how this lie will unfold.

"I'm sorry baby. I meant KFC. Now can we go? I need to get back and drop something off."

I boast, "I can take her home."

Joe responds with a familiar, "whatever." He walks away immediately making a phone call.

"Fey, I think he is into something illegal. I have a feeling."

"Anni, I have the same feeling. I hired a private detective months ago. I need a paper trail so I can get custody of Kerrigan."

"Fey, I'm so proud of you. I was beginning to wonder about you. Oppression does not suit you. Depression doesn't look good on you either. I know people go through PTSD (Post-Traumatic Stress Disorder) after ordeals. You just didn't seem like yourself, but you've been on top of things the entire time.

"Anni, I have a paper trail of at least a dozen affairs, gambling, and negligence at work. He would appear at work and then sneak out to have affairs. One woman was giving him money! The house is in his name. So, no worries."

"Fey, I knew you wouldn't let someone treat you like that. You're a genius," I happily commented.

"I knew I had to be careful and keep quiet so Kerrigan wouldn't be hurt in the process. I don't want the courts to send her to just anybody. I contacted her biological mother. She was forced into giving her up. Joe was blackmailing her. The plan is to get temporary custody awarded to me. Then, her biological mother can step back in. Keep your fingers crossed Anni."

"Fey, I'm speechless. I'm so honored to call you my friend. You would go through such lengths, with your health, for this child. You should have been a lawyer, instead of a nurse. Then again, it is your nurturing side that allows you to care so much for this child. If I ever have a baby, you will be the godmother.

"Anni, I would be delighted. Now let's find Celeste and fill her in."

Celeste is on speaker phone screaming the details of the wedding. Fey heightens the conversation at every chance with her story about Joe. The story conjures several memories for me as I'm sure Joe is into something illegal. This painful intuition is familiar to me and it's stabbing me in the gut again! I always felt my ex Jax was up to something when we were together. He would mask his endeavors with concerts or some kind of tour. Somehow, I knew, but the thrills always lasted longer than the uncertainty. That sultry life was intoxicating but also suffocating. I couldn't breathe easy with Jax. The memories flood me and I instantly seem to be in some sort of mirage. I can't breathe, my thoughts are jumbled. I feel trapped so I pull over to get some air.

"Anni, are you ok? Anni, are you ok?" Fey questioned me but her voice seemed so far away. I could hear Celeste's speaker phone voice as well! "Anni, are you ok?"

I feel as if I am back in CPR training where they reference the dummy as "Annie" and repeatedly ask if she is ok before administering CPR.

"Anni, I think you're having a panic attack!" Fey blasts!

She throws out the leftovers from the restaurant and hands me the bag. Standing on the side of the road wearing the new designer labels Baby gave me, my heels sink in the grass while I'm breathing into this greasy, brown paper bag. My ego now needs CPR.

Celeste's voice comes through the phone again, louder than ever. "Fey is she ok?"

"Fey, tell Celeste that I am fine." I demanded.

Fey instantly tells Celeste to calm down and that things were ok.

"Anni, what were you thinking about that threw you into such a mode?" Fey inquires.

"Nothing... Nothing... I'll be fine. I just needed some air. Let's get in the car and go. I'm exhausted."

Those thoughts of Jax did a number on my psyche. That was a time of panic and stroke level worry. I look over at Fey and wonder what she is really going through behind closed doors. She smiles at me and eases my mind. I drop Fey at home in hopes that Joe doesn't top off the evening with some stupid display. She walks in with no complaints.

Finally home. What a day! I got my assignment for Alec's and Celeste's wedding, "Wedding Coordinator." It sounds so much better than "Bridesmaid". Fey would settle into the Bridesmaid role. Celeste blurted this all out over the speaker phone while Fey was telling her "Joe" story. They went back and forth with news until Fey's story forced me to concentrate on my past which ended the day in a panic attack. As unsettling as the episode was, it could not tamper with the joy I felt waking up to the perfect man this morning. He dramatically displayed his feelings for me and that weighed on my mind all day.

Thoughts of Baby invade me. I remember feeling so comfortable, or was I in beautiful danger? I had the physical willingness to endure this. However, is my mind capable? Every day I would get a text from Baby. We were both so busy but managed to get to know one another better. He already knew some of my favorite things, due to Fey informing him of my love for fruit and my favorite hazelnut and chocolate candy. He had such an interest in pleasing me. I embraced it.

A week passed and I needed to see him. So, I accepted his invitation. I invited him over. He arrived with my favorite candy, a bottle of wine and an orchid. I am so pleased with the sight of this man that the gifts stood in the background. We talked for hours. His life had been a series of events planned by his parents. My life would be the opposite. My rebellion drove Ma and Rich insane. If they wanted my hair straightened, I wore it curly. I was laid back and Baby was straight forward. He dreamed of driving a fancy car and I wanted to ride a bike around the world. Baby was a lot like Alec. My parents set Alec and Celeste up but knew I would never be introduced to an arrangement of a marriage. Plans can fall through and then life gets in the way of actually "living". I love life entirely too much. I was whimsical and free flowing. Celeste just happened to be a perfect mate for my brother. She seemed to think he imprinted on her, as they say wolves do. My mate would have to mirror my passion for life. I wanted to be "fed" instead of "served".

The next few months would prove to be just that. Baby gave me "living": random runs for ice cream, gift deliveries, late night talks and walks. During one of our walks, Baby and I got lost in conversation and aimlessly stumbled upon a playground. We channeled our playful sides. We took turns on the slide. I was wearing a dress so Baby took off his shirt so I could sit on it and slide down without hurting my legs. When I got to the bottom, he was waiting with a kiss. He escorted me to the swings. We both sat down in separate swings and locked legs with each other. I could not look at him another moment without his shirt on. I got up and gave it to him and he stood up and put his shirt on but began to unbutton his pants. While kissing me, he picks me up and sits back down on the swing with me sitting on top of him. We began to swing. Each time in the air was mind blowing. I held on to him tight and enjoyed the ride. I was weak with fulfillment. He actually carried me on his back most of the way home. I slept the night away, in his arms. I thought moments like these would slow down with the holiday season approaching. The Townsend family was always busy during that time of year. The charities and workshops were demanding. However, Baby and I still found time to spend together. He helped pass out turkeys for Thanksgiving and to distribute toys for Christmas. We were devoted to the romance.

Each time I saw him, I became more addicted. I was like a kid in a candy store. Ironically, that was my Valentine's gift. We crashed a candy store. Baby was friends with the owner and had it closed down an hour early so I could have my way. When in actuality, he had his way with me. I'll never look at another candy store quite the same. I was addicted to him and couldn't focus.

The spring charity event was sponsored by a couple who would make an actual physical appearance this year, instead of just writing a check. Zora Hughes always donated, and this year she would make an appearance with her husband, Neale, for the kids. This would be my first meeting with the Hughes. I had to make a good impression.

Baby had captured me and was claiming my time. Whenever I didn't speak with him, it altered my day. I had become dependent on him. I couldn't stand myself any longer. I had to discuss this with Fey and Celeste and arrange a self-intervention.

Chapter 3

My menu for the girls...

- Pan seared salmon (marinated with Coke and soy sauce)
- Brown rice
- Zucchini matchsticks
- Sweet potatoes topped with melted marshmallows and chopped pecans.
- Ginger punch (Hennessey, apple juice, slice of pineapple with the juice and a Ginger stick), a definite truth serum for the evening.

The farmers market is busy, but I need to grab my zucchini and also fruit for a platter. I get the urge for sugar snap peas... I reach over to grab them and the arm that reaches over mine has a snake with red eyes on it... Can't be!! I follow the long muscular arm up to the face and it indeed belongs to my ex, Jax. Jaxon Stone...

"So, you cook now?" he probed.

"Anni, it's never too late to learn! I'm still trying to master your technique with the peas. Nobody does it like you do".

"Good luck with that. Take care."

"Wait, Doll. Teach me the right way... we could catch up. It'll be fun."

"Jax, it wasn't fun then and it won't be fun now."

"Doll, I've changed." I'm not that night owl anymore. My saxophone is only used to teach now. I'm a music teacher."

"Congrats to you, Jax." Send my love to your mother." I follow with a simple kiss on the cheek as a salutation.

He forces out a "Goodbye, Doll."

Jax was a self-named ladies' man. But he said I wasn't just a lady. I was a doll; made to perfection and I should be put on the shelf until he was ready for me. Sad thing is... he actually thought I would wait for him to finish portraying himself as the sexy saxophonist of the night, playing his tune to any woman who would listen. I actually met Jax at the cafe during an Eric Roberson set. The same café where Baby saved me in the parking lot. His voice was a mixture of heaven and hell... His songs were handpicked for each woman. He wrote for them and then he wrote them off. They never saw it coming. However, he warned me and asked me to be his doll. I'm not anyone's "doll". We became friends and fell into a relationship. But something was missing. We had some intense times but I spent most of the time trying to figure out what was missing.

Baby was what was missing.... Hmm...

Revelation on aisle 5!

My little trip down memory lane today will prove entertaining for the ladies tonight. Dinner is about ready! Celeste arrives first. She looks amazing even in a sundress with her red hair in a bun... The homemade bag of bread she's holding smells just as amazing as she looks.

She blurts out, "Anni, I'm excited about the wedding but I think Alec may have cold feet. He has been very distant during the planning."

"My dear, let's examine what you just said... you're excited about the wedding. Shouldn't you be excited about your marriage?"

"Damnit, I've been here two minutes and you've already solved my problem! How do you do it?"

"Wait, I didn't solve anything. I just know brides. You get caught up in the bride "role" and forget about the wife "position." Let Alec know there is life after the wedding. Men want to feel needed. Being a bride is temporary. A wife should be permanent. It's a way of life. It should be forever. It's why I'm having a hard time understanding how Baby could have a "play wife." She must be pretty addicted to fame not to want love. I mean, I know some marriages don't work out, but to go into it knowing it has no backbone... it's bound to fall apart."

"Anni, he loves you. He could never tell you because you were preoccupied with Jax."

"Celeste!" I abruptly interrupted. "I saw Jax today!"

He invited me to "catch up". I walked away from the invite with no problem. I realized it never worked out because he wasn't Baby.

"Anni, Jax is gorgeous and has the voice of an angel but if you hadn't traveled all over the country with the sexy saxophonist, you probably would have realized Baby was going to marry the ice princess".

"The ice princess?" I chuckled.

"She's a walking jewelry box, Anni. She plays tennis wearing actual diamond tennis bracelets. It makes her feel pretty."

I was laughing so hard I almost didn't hear the doorbell.

Fey walked right in... "Let's eat! I brought Chocolate too. You guys look great."

Fey always looks pulled together. No one ever knows when she is sick. She's not the "victim" type. She's wearing a beautiful black dress that flows from her medium build and she is wearing short hair today. Fey would surprise us with different hairstyles via wigs or weaves. She had a beautiful head of hair but had a phobia that her hair would one day fall out due to illness. Therefore, she was training herself to adapt. She always had a plan.

"Fey, Anni saw Jax today."

"Really! How did that go Anni?"

"He was charming and asked for a date."

"What did you say?"

"I let him down easy. I even kissed him on the cheek."

"Anni, you know that was just fuel, right? It gives him hope. You should have just given him the old pat on the back."

"Hmm... Maybe you're right. I was thinking it was kind of a *good-bye forever* gesture... After being apart for so long, I could see how a

ɹld make our agreement seem null and void. We agreed to
. be romantic again. The romance altered our friendship and I
wanted to leave everything that happened with Jax in the past. I just
offered a simple kiss on the cheek as a final salutation. I imagine he
wouldn't feed into it."

Fey exclaims "Of course he will feed into it. He's a man! All they
need is one little crumb of hope to feed on."

"I don't have anything left for him Fey. Well, maybe one little
crumb of this bread Celeste brought tonight. He can feed off that."
Laughter enters the room and pulls up a chair because it's going to be
here for a while. We laughed right through dinner and right through
clean up. Carefully, avoiding chipping a nail, Celeste loads the dish-
washer and Fey is bagging up leftovers when she says, "Anni, the food
was delightful! Have you cooked for Baby yet?"

Celeste adds, "Yes, have you?"

"Why do the two of you act as if Baby and I are just dating? He's a
married man and we're sneaking around!"

Fey boasts, "Anni, have you ever felt like he was sneaking with
you? He doesn't seem to mind being seen with you."

"I don't know. I never feel like the other woman until he leaves
me. If it was all about me, he wouldn't leave?" I surrender to a visual
orgasm every time I look at him. However, I know he has other obli-
gations and that's a hard pill to down.

"Fey, give it to her. Give her the envelope."

"What the hell are you two up to now?"

I open a beautiful card with two plane tickets to Hawaii inside!

Fey screaming, "Anni, he asked us to give it to you so you wouldn't be compelled to decline instantly!"

"Do you two work for him or something? You were supposed to come over and talk me out of this."

Celeste grabs their coats and the chocolate! "We're going to a movie. You are going to get ready because Baby will be here at 9 sharp." They giggle their way out of the door and leave me hanging while holding these tickets in my hand. They set me up. So much for a girl's night.

A knock on the door? He's really early. I look through the peep hole and a beautiful blue orchid is staring me in the face.

"Delivery for Ms. Townsend"

"Yes. I'm Ms. Townsend"

"Sign here, please."

The card reads, "It was lovely seeing you today, Doll."

Hells no... It's from Jax. The kiss on the cheek must have been fuel. The same man who once told me he had to rush home because he left his candles burning is trying to seduce me.

My laughter is interrupted by my phone ringing.

"Baby calling," my phone reads.

I answer, "Hawaii, huh?"

"You always wanted to go. I want to share that with you. I want to kiss you for days and just create a rhythm without any interruptions. I'll be there shortly so we can practice... "

"Just kissing, huh?"

Baby, seduction is an art. A true Artisan is supposed to work with his hands."

"I plan to use my hands as well. I can mold you into quite a knot my dear. I can make you curl up into a ball with just my fingers. Pressing, rolling you around, and using my other hand to be careful not to lose form. Folding you until I get the right angle... I will try all angles until I reach that perfect niche... crosshatching your legs until your face reaches the perfect low value of blushing red. There. That smile. A masterpiece...

"Open the door gorgeous... I couldn't wait... I'm here."

My art lesson is on the other side of this door... I open the door and immediately think; "now that's how you seduce a girl!" I didn't stand a chance... I buckled right there in front of the fireplace and he began to teach me. I obeyed every step and welcomed every process. Indeed a masterpiece! We slept at the very spot.

Morning comes and I think of words and how I've never cooked for him... It's my turn to make a masterpiece.

- Spinach
- Mushrooms
- Tomatoes
- Eggs

Omelet it is!

I take turkey bacon slices and arrange them in a skillet with a lattice technique (like a pie crust) in a different skillet, I sautéed the veggies with butter and olive oil next... spinach goes in last.

I form the omelet with eggs, white cheese blend and cream. I mix in some of the veggies...

I plate the omelet and top it with turkey bacon. I arranged it in lattice form so it doesn't slide off the top. I add remaining veggies and drizzle it butter, cream, and cheese mixture. I give him a bowl made from a cantaloupe with fresh fruit inside, dusted with powdered sugar to balance out the savory omelet.

The smell awakened him already but he comes over and admits to the sight of me cooking awakening another part of him. He places me on the counter and begins to feed me a strawberry... Then takes a bite himself all while his appetite for me is growing... He kisses me after every bite he takes... I'm going to come off this counter. I'm amazed at his appetite for me. He is feasting from below my waist. I lose my-self... We actually go to the bed after... breakfast!

I slept the morning away. He's like a sleeping pill... I wake up to an easel and art supplies. He was sketching me while I slept... He kept the supplies in his car. A true artist is always ready because we feed from the passion. You could not tell by this beautiful canvas of a man himself that he led his life with a gavel instead of a paintbrush. He was so talented. I barely got out of the bed. We ate the remains of the fruit from breakfast and made love all day. We managed a shower together and a few more rounds of pure indulgence... I was high from him. I had to sleep... He ordered food in and we watched a movie. The movie actually watched us. We were exhausted. He spent the entire weekend at my cozy little place. After changing a few light bulbs and bagging up the trash, he noticed my new blue orchid. He commented on how the girls must have given it to me until he read the card.

"Jaxon? Anni, really?"

"Baby, I saw him at the farmer's market and he sent over the orchid a few hours later.

"I see. What was your natural reaction to him, gorgeous? Be honest."

"Baby, I realized that things didn't work out with him simply because he wasn't you. He doesn't do it for me like you do. You send chills all over me. I get a surge just from thinking of you."

"Anni, I want you to be mine... I know someone will come into your life and sweep you off of your feet and that's the part about this that eats at me the most. I'm going to take this orchid out with the trash."

The jealousy was concerning. What does he expect me to do? I can't put a halt to my life and wait for him to decide if he wants a real marriage or continue this... this... I don't even know what this is... Does he think I'm a doll, too?

"I'm not going to go run off into the sunset with Jax. I shiver at the thought. Baby, I'm taking this one day at a time. I don't know what may come. I'm trying to conquer this unsettling feeling of needing you all the time. I never felt this need for Jax or anyone else. Let's deal with you and I. Don't worry about Jax.

I struggle with the need to be next to you at all times. It makes me feel bad to want you."

"Anacelia, I want you to want me. I want you to feel for me. All this time, I wondered... my mind took little snapshots of you and I would replay them at the most inopportune moments. I'd smile sitting at a stop light. Once, staring at a dollar bill, in a checkout line, I smiled hopelessly. That night years ago when we were in the cafe, I asked if you believed in God, you took the waitresses tip and circled the words, IN GOD WE TRUST. You've even changed the way I look at money."

He walked over and pulled out his wallet. He gives me a folded dollar bill... He kept it! He kept the same dollar bill from that night. The words were circled in bright blue ink... I also colored in the eye in the pyramid, blue, like his eyes, as a joke.

"Baby, I had no idea. I just don't know what to do with you. I now think of you being married at those same inopportune moments. When I'm pumping gas... When I'm brushing my hair... The thought creeps into my life during my everyday tasks. I wonder how things would be if you weren't married. I'm fighting myself. I want to think this is ok based on the circumstances involving the reason you got married, but no matter what, I think I'm a horrible person because of it. She has no idea. She will be hurt. I don't want to cause anyone pain."

"Gorgeous, don't worry about Ivy. She will be fine."

"Baby, Ivy is just a woman. I'm not worried about her. She bleeds just as I do. I'm worried about a higher power. How will the heavens ever reward me if I continue this? This is a big deal to me."

"Anni, I carry the burden as well. The heavens have provided you with love and compassion. Only you can hold such placement of a heart that big. You shall be rewarded. I believe that. Thank you for acknowledging my illness toward the situation. I know you don't have to pacify me, but it matters that you explained his acts to me. If he presents a problem to your well-being, you will inform me?

"Yes, I will call you to save the day."

"Anni, no jokes!"

"Yes, you will be the first to know."

"Come let me hold you. I have to go."

He wraps me up. In those arms I've gotten quite familiar.

"It's been a most wonderful weekend. I don't want to leave you but I have to prepare for work." I sighed as he wrapped me deeper into his loving arms.

Chapter 4

Annie, will you come get me?

Frantically asking, "Fey, is that you? What's wrong?"

"I've been arrested. I can't bond until tomorrow."

"Are you ok? Can you tell me what happened?"

"There was an argument at the house. Joe swung to hit me. I moved and he fell down the stairs. I ran out of the house to my sister's place. I should have gone to the police first. Joe got bruises from his fall. He told the police that his bruises stemmed from me hitting him with an object. They believed him because I didn't have any visible injuries or bruises. They arrested me on the spot. I have to stay overnight."

"Anni, he's a coward. He lied to prevent himself from going to jail. He attacked me! I've never felt like this before. In one instance, my freedom was taken from me and I was innocent. The police and the justice system have failed me. He attacked me and they protected him. I'm going to need Alec to be my lawyer. Please cover for me at work."

"Of course, I'll inform him. We will be there first thing tomorrow morning."

"Ok, I have to go. They should let me go at.....

The phone shuts off...

She was sobbing; the man who should love and protect her was destroying her. His manipulative ways are countless. I can only imagine going through that. She was a loving, caring woman who was raising another woman's child, her husband's child. Joe had been the worst man I'd ever come to meet. He was all smiles and jokes but was a spineless narcissist in real time. She even found out he didn't know how to write a check. His answer to this was "I only deal with cash money." Classic behavior of a two bit hustler who was morally bankrupt. He was resting in their six bedroom house while she was sitting in a cell sobbing, sharing her space with real criminals. What idiot cop would put her in jail? He must be some crooked bastard linked to Joe in some illegal madness. Some "no character" fool who suffered from some sort of malfunction. He probably couldn't get it up or his parents were cousins or something. His only purpose in life was to make people suffer to match his own inside battle. Joe probably found out what Fey was up to and called in this terror of a favor. I hope she is safe. Alec will take care of her.

"Alec, sorry to wake you... Something terrible has happened."

Morning comes and we don't know what time to get her. We went early with a bondsman. We're not sure of the charges. Alec thinks that a domestic charge would consist of a twelve-hour hold. Alec is livid. He hates Joe. We waited for hours... She came out with swollen eyes from crying all night. She had slippers on because she ran to her sister's place as she was. I still can't believe she went to the police for protection and was arrested. I was so upset. I had a knot in my throat and hate in my veins. I took her to my place to rest. I went to work to take care of the patient load. She would be safe at my place. Fey was my friend but also my co-worker and I wanted to make sure she was covered at work.

Alec was a passionate lawyer. He believed in justice. We got permission from Fey to go and retrieve her things. We took a deputy with us. Joe was not the kind of man who would just let us in. Joe was powerless to Alec and the deputy. This inferior feeling fueled a lot of his bad decisions... a result of fruitlessness working on a weak mind again. He was a terrible person. Alec directed Fey to get a restraining order and she complied. The loss of control would build up within Joe and turn into pure anger. He showed up at my home to see her and tried to attack her. Fey called 911. I called Alec and Baby. This act would prove that he was the aggressor. Rich, my stepfather, also showed up under the direction of Alec.

All of the men in my life had been there to show Fey that she was a part of our family. All standing there with two cops, Joe didn't stand a chance. He was arrested on site. His charges were trespassing and not obeying a restraining order. The officers were real policemen; men of honor. Joe would now see how it felt to sleep in a jail. Fey walks over saying, "The restraining order worked. You're brilliant. Thanks Alec." Rich adds, "Fey, you are my daughter as well. You can always call if you need anything."

"Thanks Mr. Townsend."

My Baby stood in the shadows making several phone calls. Rich wasn't sure why Baby was there. He is Alec's best friend so he didn't question it. Rich requests that Fey come to stay with him and Ma Ma. My mother of Latin decent would shower her with rich food and affection. Fey agreed to stay.

"Baby girl, will you be ok? Maybe Alec should stay with you a few days. Alec, stay with your sister."

"Dad, I'll take care of her."

Alec always called Rich, Dad. I always called him Rich. It just kind of worked out like that.

We all hugged Fey and assured her things will turn out ok.

I'm exhausted. Baby offers to stay with me so Alec could flee to Celeste. I'm sure she's a wreck right now. I go inside to call her and fill her in.

"Alec, Can I talk to you while Anni's inside? I arranged for Fey to stay at the condo. She can take a leave of absence from work and won't have any concerns of him showing up at her workplace. Now he knows there is a protective order in place and he will be sneakier with his antics."

"What are you two whispering about?" I ask.

"We will work it all out," Alec says. He leaves us to go comfort his fiancé as I just told her he was on his way.

Sitting on the sofa, I thank Baby for being there. I'm one lucky gal to have so much love around me. Fey wasn't so lucky. Her family was distant and at times non- existent. Her father was dead and her mother was always preoccupied with anything other than family.

Baby never held me so tight. He would be sure Joe would leave Fey alone. The protective order was good for one year. We would call the P.I. that Fey hired to help the case. I had no doubt that Baby and Alec would protect her. I slept next to his rib all night.

"Good morning, gorgeous, I have to go to New York to visit my brother. Would you like to go?"

"I would love to go but I have best friend duties. Fey needs me."

"You're such a good person, gorgeous... Maybe a long weekend? Ask Fey to join. The two of you can come up. She could use some time away. A change of environment will be good."

"Okay Baby!" I'll text her...

"Fey, Baby has invited us to New York, would ya like to go?"

"Hells yea!" She replied within seconds.

"Lol... I'll send you the details."

"Well Baby, She wants to go. Let's do it!"

"Great! It will do me some good to see my brother."

I often wondered if he had adapted an accent like Baby had. "He seems interesting. You both are dangerously intriguing, two of a kind but still different."

"My mother thought it would be a good idea to give us the same name. Brothers with the same name... This would prove to be awful in adult life. It's a difficult hand to play. Having a brother with the same name plays tricks with human perception. People automatically thought we were the same person. This provoked a lot of fun when my brother learned he could utilize it to his advantage. It also doesn't help that my dad and grandfather share the name as well. My family refers to my brother as Drei (dry) which means three in German. He's the third Davenport with the name, passed down from my German great grandmother who adored it. I simply became "Baby." We represent a long line of Black Anglo-Saxons, Germans, and Brits who think racism is dead and buried. But I'm aware that it is not. I always say *it may be buried but it's not dead.* It arises and presents its ugly head more often than we acknowledge and at times in reverse. But, I love how my family sees no color. We love all and it shows through generations of the choices we have made."

"Baby, it's beautiful to just sit and listen to you tell about it."

"Gorgeous, my family has the utmost respect or the hand that feeds us and at times upholds the ideal of what we are supposed to be; an imagery of the perfect storm. They mingle, date and marry with whites to create acceptance. The naivety waves over our perception of how the world should be. We prove that you can coexist with whomever chosen. My *racism doesn't exist;* childhood groomed me to marry a white woman, as did my father. It threw me into a *situationship.* My darker skin and blue eyes cradle the *goal.* Something as simple as my eyes has defined me. Every day I get the, *black man with blue eyes,* look.

I am the epitome, the imagery of what they stand for. Therefore, I was placed on a pedestal. My brother has his own road of acceptance to travel. Drei is a genius but often feels the need to down play himself to show us he doesn't need acceptance. His nonchalant lifestyle is inviting but also quite overrated. He sleeps when he should be working and drinks when he should be sleeping."

"Yet, he still maintains a level of righteousness. He's fun to be around and I love him dearly. What's most disarming is when people stare at me, shaking their heads, insinuative of me wearing contacts to be "white". They have no clue this is the way I was designed. This burns a whole in Drei. He angers fast and his *big brother* ego always takes over.

"Baby, I've heard that birth order can affect human psychology. First born are more usually more conservative and achievement oriented and last born are more rebellious and open. But you two defy the theories."

"Yes, I guess we kind of fell into our roles based upon the situation. He settled into the rebel, care free role to protect, to always be available to me. I became the driven, political brother. I'm not much of an agreeable, people pleaser as they think last born children can be. We accept each other, bad decisions and all. I can't wait for you to meet him. I think Fey will like him."

"Fey? Baby, what are you up to?"

"I'll send you the travel info my love. Get ready for a few fun filled days. I have to get moving. I'll let you know when I arrive. Hold it in the road until then and Anacelia, thanks for rescuing me. You are just what I need around me."

He leaves me with the biggest grin on my face. I sat for moments thinking about a possible life with this man...

Who could be knocking at the door? I wondered...

"Did you leave something Baby?"

"No, and he is not leaving me either!"

"Ivy!! Hells no..."

"Mrs. Davenport to you."

"You shouldn't be here. Why *are* you here?"

"Is there another reason other than you sleeping with my husband?" she says angrily.

"Ivy, I know of your arrangement, your contentment deal."

"Anacelia, what you're not aware of is that I indeed love my husband."

"Oh, you mean the *Philia* type reduction of love, the dispassionate form of whatever you're holding on to for personal gain, that kind of love?" I added sarcastically.

"Anacelia, I'm aware that he feels a different love for you. A love that makes him say your name while he's sleeping, which led me right to you. A love without logic... Thriving off of emotion and longing has neither no place in politics nor law. Your erotic or *Eros* type of love will cause you to think you can have my husband. My love is better suited for him. I was handpicked for him and I will push him to be great. "

"Ivy, you've pushed him so hard, he stumbled right over me. I picked him up and now he can clearly see where he is going. He *is* on the right path."

"Anacelia, your emotions are deciding your words. When you would like to speak with me about your affair with my husband, contact me. You owe me an explanation. I'll be waiting."

I've never taken such pride in slamming a door. Ugh. This woman has nerves of steel! Maybe she's on to something, though. The passion could be our only fuel. He's addicted to the romance because he's been without it. Further examination could give me some insight. Her words are designed by her thoughts. My words are designed by my emotions. I knew I wasn't thinking this through. I wanted to tell him she came to see me but I can't. He would be broken if he thought my livelihood was in danger.

Another passenger just got invited on the NY trip. Awkwardness would surely sit next to me. I can't tell Celeste. She is very protective; she would crack and tell Alec. I had to call Fey and fill her in on what Ivy said to me on her visit and how I would use the trip to gauge my relationship with Baby. Is it just the sex? It would be one hotel room on this trip, for me and Fey to share. Baby can stay with Drei. A "no intimacy" trip... Can I manage this? He knows all the switches to turn me on. I'm up to the challenge. New York, here we come.

I didn't know if I would crumple or not. But first further examination... Where are my shoes?

Do I hear Baby's voice? Where am I? How did I get here? I slept outside. What the hell is going on? My clothes are drenched. Surely, it's from the sprinkler system on this massive property. Why is my memory so fuzzy? It appears to be an empty bottle of Hennessy next to me. However, it's not really empty because it holds the explanation for me being here. My head feels like Gabby Douglas has been flipping through it all night. *Think Anni!* I must have followed Ivy home... Oh great! I hear voices uttering something about someone in jail... Maybe this door will stash me away. Oh wow! The room has some kind of ensuite. This must be a guest house. I'm assuredly not a guest in Baby's and Ivy's home, but the voices seem closer so I jump in the bed to pretend to be asleep. Maybe if they think I'm a guest, they will leave and I can dash out of here. The door opens and some guy says, "I saw this empty bottle on the grounds so I started inspecting. "Do you know her?"

"Yes, I know her." *Baby's voice! The butterflies start to stir...*

"Should I speak with Ms. Ivy as well?"

"No, there is no need. Carry on."

"Anacelia, why are you here? You're soaked!"

"That bottle of Hennessy and I apparently took a cab here last night. I don't know why I'm here." *I couldn't bring myself to tell him Ivy came to see me.*

"You have no idea where you are. This is Ivy's suite. She sleeps here."

The butterflies in my stomach now feel like bees swarming. My jumping into Ivy's bed must have triggered the hired hand's suspicion even more. "Baby, get me out of here."

"Here Anni, Let's get you something to wear. "He pulls out an Ivory cashmere trench coat, trimmed in pink. The tags were still in place. He drapes it over me and we head to the back of the property. He calls for a car.

"You sleep in different beds? In totally different structures?"

"Anacelia, I've told you of our arrangement."

"Yes, but Baby she loves you."

"Gorgeous, she loves the idea of me. We tried to have a romantic relationship but it just didn't work. I don't sleep with her. I don't dream of her. I dream of you. I can't wait for our New York getaway so that I can spend more time with you. I'm going to ride home with you."

We both get in the car and he holds me like I might run away. Nobody holds me like this man.

"Anacelia, I know this has to be hard for you. But you don't need to parade around in the middle of the night searching for my heart. My heart doesn't live at that house. My heart lives with you."

"Baby, the rest of you lives at that house."

Chapter 5

I didn't know what to expect from this trip. But, it was all that I hoped. We paraded all around New York. Drei was a great host and easy on the eyes, or, in Fey's words, "Were these men made in a factory?" I caught Drei staring at Fey a few times. Standing tall, with long coarse black hair and Grand Marnier colored skin, Fey was quite the looker. Drei looked as if he wanted to drink her. We had exquisite food and the shopping in Soho was magnificent. We marched from borough to borough. Harlem had the most beautiful brownstones. When we walked, Baby walked next to the street, opened my doors and stood up on the train, so I could sit. Chivalry still exists. He even stood in front of me when a bus hurried past and threw a puddle of water at us. We sat on the same side of the table like teenagers and always ordered different things so we could share. Our first meal consisted of oxtails and jerk chicken. At dinner, he leaned over and cupped my hands, discussing the night before.

The white, waving tablecloth creating a barrier, surrendered my need for him. I pulled back my hands because his were carrying an electric current. The surge was traveling through me. All I could think of was leaving to roll around in a set of sheets that resembled the restaurant's preventative tablecloth. My mind was so far from the meal. If he kept touching me, this "no intimacy" trip was going to hell in a hand basket quick. I had been to New York but only on a tour guided trip. This trip proved different. The air here was different. I could hear people thinking of their hopes and dreams.

My mind keeps swaying back to the Brownstones in Harlem. They were monumental. The atmosphere around the Apollo Theatre took me to a different era. I could hear music in the streets and envisioned people wearing their best for a night out. My daydreaming was in rare form. I gathered that the streets were full of laughter and togetherness back then until I was interrupted by several passers-by with far away looks in their eyes. A sea of Zombie like people was all around me. The realistic atmosphere consisted of an intense sense of hustling and receiving.

I felt blessed to be on the inside of a time capsule that had come to life in Manhattan. Time Square's eye catching lights seemed like a subtle daydream compared to the glow I see around Baby when I look at him. He was wearing a body halo. Baby and I were able to let go and be our selves. We talked and laughed. He comforted me with words alone. Holding my hand through the sea of fast paced moguls was just one memory I had. Dozens include sharing a delicious pizza that made me hive due to the pork content. He held me and fed me Benadryl saying, "Out of all things to be allergic to. I now know why you pre-pared turkey bacon the other morning," he says laughing. In the same breath, he utters, " You're hives make you even more beautiful. It tells a story and proves that you are just human. Your imperfections are perfect."

New York provided some comfort in this *situationship* with Baby. However, my relationship with New York had completely changed. I was in love with the city. I saw it with fresh eyes. Ivy may have been wrong. Our love contained the ingredients needed to make a life together and this trip was my major deciding factor to carry on. I decided right then and there that I would accompany Baby to Hawaii. It would be more time alone to figure us out.

Fey was having the time of her life. After all, that's what the trip was really about. Our little field trip took Fey's mind off of Joe until the court appearances. Fey's court date comes up and all charges are thrown out due to Joe coming to my place, proving he was the aggressor, just days after Fey was arrested. Joe's court date approached. He was furious as the judge ruled that he would have to attend anger management and parenting courses at Fey's request. Joe was also charged with filing a false police report, domestic violence, trespassing, not obeying a protective order, and was assigned a probation officer. He would also enter a drug rehab program as he failed a drug screen given by his P.O. Joe's ego stepped in majorly. All of these labels didn't fit into his "want to be" status. He was fine with his uncontrollable fits as long as people didn't know who he really was. He couldn't hide it anymore. People laughed at him. People judged him. We hoped he would get the help he needed. His daughter deserved better. With

Joe in rehab, someone had to take care of Kerrigan. Fey stepped in. She was the closest thing she had to a parent right now. Fey exhausted finances paying for a new home and car. The car had been lost to the bankruptcy. She had been living off a five dollar a day budget with meals consisting of hot pockets and pop tarts while she saved for her home and the car. Tuition for Kerrigan didn't come easy. We had no idea until her sister told us she was struggling with finances. Fey would never tell us of any financial troubles. She was a strong willed woman, a *"pay my own bills"* kind of woman. But I'm not taking no for an answer. I'll get Ma to baby sit Kerrigan and I will give her a little monetary gift and plan a girl's day. I needed things for Hawaii! Great time for a shopping trip...

We take Kerrigan to my parents. Ma Ma is so happy to babysit. She takes Kerrigan to the kitchen to get a snack.

"Princesita, go to the fridge and pick out a snack."

Kerrigan screams, "I CAN? May I get a snack for Fey? She never gets a snack." She usually watches me eat and says *"I'll just have a big hug for a snack."* Sometimes she even says she will take a big hug and a kiss for dinner. Then she says, "That's all I need."

"Ay dios mio... Mi Princesita..." says Mrs. Townsend.

"Fey is a really good mommy, huh? You get as many snacks as you want! Would you like to help me prepare a lunch Princesita?"

"Yes ma'am. Can we make Tacos?"

"Yes, anything for you." Says Ma Ma.

Entering the kitchen, we thank Ma Ma for taking care of Kerrigan.

"No problem Niña. May I talk with you please? Over here!"

"Ma Ma what's wrong?"

"Anacelia, I don't think Fey has been eating regularly. She has been giving her portions to the child. Please talk to her today and make sure they are ok. I will make a basket for them to take home, just as a gift. Please tell Fey that she can return here to stay if she pleases."

"Que vamos a hacer si sucede algo?"

I hug her. "Ma Ma todo estara bien."

"Mrs. Townsend, Thank you for babysitting Kerri for me."

"Con mucho gusto, Fey—Go! Have Fun! We will have the fun here. Go! Go!"

We go say goodbye to Rich. He is sitting in his favorite chair.

"Girls, it's so good to see you. You both look beautiful. Where is my daughter-n-law to be?"

"We are going to pick up Celeste now Mr. Townsend."

"Give her my best, Fey. How are things?" He probes.

"I'm taking it one day at a time, sir."

"Well, take this day and enjoy it. The little one will be fine here. It will do us some good to practice being grandparents. I would like to think our children will bless us with grandkids one day. I thought that Jaxon guy would stay around…

"RICH!" I noticed the smirk and side eye…

Ma Ma does indeed look happy in that kitchen. They will probably bake everything in sight!

"We will be back in a few hours."

We said our goodbyes and Fey was calling back to my parent's house before we got to the stop sign at the corner.

"Fey, put the phone down. You will give her a false sense of something being wrong if you overload her with calls. Children notice patterns."

"Ok. I won't call. She's been through so much. My worry intensified when I ran across something she wrote…"

"What did she write Fey?"

"I have it with me. I keep it in my purse…"

FREE YOURSELF

That little girl wants to come out

She's afraid to play

Hiding inside… care free is not in her vocabulary

She doesn't understand… only a moderate form of amusement has graced her existence…

She missed it… her childhood

Her chance may be gone….

Though her willingness to be happy stands strong

She would one day smile on the inside

Her pride will take a seat

And allow her soft side to stand
She will be freed

"Fey that was beautiful! She has such a profound vocabulary to be so young."

"I gave her a poetry book at an early age. I also taught her to write her thoughts down so she will be fully able to articulate and express herself when she becomes a young woman. The books are just fuel for her talent. She has a gift! Listen to this piece…"

DROWNING

The ceiling is open
But the walls are too tall to climb out
There is a way out
But I just can't make it
It's too hard
It all caught me off guard
I sit in here with my troubles
As they can't escape either
I have shelter but the elements can still get in
I'm still affected by the storm
Then I realize
Use the umbrella

Use the rain coat or a floating device

GOD provided me with tools to weather the storm.

Be patient and stick it out

It rained and it rained... and it rained

Just when I thought I was going to drown...

The rain made the water so high that I could swim to the top

I was free. The rain had become a wonderful sound

No more walls

What could have killed me was the same thing that rescued me.

"She's never had grandparents. She will really enjoy today." Fey replied.

"Fey, children are resilient. The only thing on her mind today will be cookies and candy. She will be treated like a princess at the Townsend house. She may even speak Spanish when we get back!"

Our laughter is so loud; we hardly hear my phone ring...

"Hi, Celeste."

"Where are you guys?"

"We're almost there." I report.

"What's your ETA?"

"Celeste, kill the military OCD'ness... We'll be there soon."

"Ok. Hurry! I have to gossip!"

We pull up and Celeste runs to the car screaming... "I saw Jax! I saw Jax!"

"What? Celeste calm down." Fey demands.

"Are you sure it was him?" I ask.

"Yes, Anni, I recognized that silly tattoo. He owns his own event space now, catering, live music—the works! He recognized me and wanted to speak only of you of course. He wants you to go into business with him. I think he called you an event guru. However, he is afraid to speak with you about it."

"Celeste, he should be afraid. That will never work and I thought he was a music teacher now?'

"Anni Townsend! Are you going to sit back and wait for Baby to decide on what he wants?"

"Celeste, this isn't about Baby by comparison. It's about Jax. I can't depend on Jax. He is unpredictable and so far away from being reliable that the man would need a passport just to make a promise. Those lies have traveled so far around the world that there has to be some still out there waiting to catch up with him.

"Maybe you should hear him out. What could it hurt?" Celeste asks.

"Whose phone is ringing?" Fey asks as she scrambles through her purse.

"Hello. Yes, this is Fedan."

I can't wait for Fey's phone call to end so Celeste would stop speaking to me about Jax.

"Fey, is everything ok?" I ask.

"That was Kerrigan's mom, Andrea. She wants to meet. I told her I was busy."

"Fey, if you need to see her, we can arrange something. Please call her back."

Celeste agrees.

Fey calls her back to set up something. Celeste is never this quiet. We both listen to the call...

"Ladies, can we meet her today?" Fey hopefully asks.

"Yes, yes." We agreed.

"She seems like a nice person. This should be interesting." Fey informs us that Andrea will meet us for lunch."

I have to speak to Fey about what Ma Ma said today. There is no easy way to do it. So, I dived right in.

"Fey, will Andrea have the means to take care of Kerrigan on her own?"

"We've talked about it briefly. She has a lot of family who can step in and help. They've been waiting on this moment. It is indeed hard to take care of a child on one income. Kerrigan and I are having current battles but it's manageable. I have ways to get by."

"Get by? What do you mean Fey? Celeste asks."

"Sometimes I take diet supplements to suppress my hunger. I stick to the budget so Kerrigan can have the extra fun kid stuff. I'm not proud to say I skip meals but I don't want her to be tainted by any of this. I don't have much of an appetite most days anyway. I chose not to turn the gas on in the warm months. The only things in the house that run by gas are the heating and the oven. I use a portable grill and microwave to prepare meals. We eat a lot of fresh foods as well."

"Fey, you don't have to sacrifice like this. We are your friends. Allow us to help you."

"You guys I'm not poor. I just have a few tricks to make ends meet every month. If I stick to the tricks, I don't have to ask for handouts."

"Fey, you didn't feel comfortable living in Baby's condo? There was no rent and that could easily help. You know he doesn't mind."

"Anni, it was a great tactic to save money. However, my pride was eating me up. I also thought of Ivy often and how she could probably toss me out at any given moment. I rather control my own situation since I have Kerrigan. I can't afford any surprises with a small child with me."

"I understand. I know it's tough out there. We will help you and not take no for an answer. You have maintenance medicine to take. You CANNOT miss meals.

"Anni…"

Celeste interrupts her, "Fey we will help you and that's final"… She reaches from the backseat and turns the song's volume up over Fey's attempts to speak. Fey has been defeated. Off to lunch to meet Andrea.

Andrea is a beautiful one. She is very well spoken and poised, nothing of the picture Joe has painted. She was respectful and very gracious toward Fey. I guess she would be to the woman who has been raising her child.

"Ladies, thank you for meeting me on short notice. My lawyer said time is running out and we need to act while Joe is still in rehab. Joe took Kerrigan from me during one of his family gatherings. The police showed up making accusations of me abusing her. His family pretended to be witnesses to such abuse and I was arrested. He didn't care of having custody of her he just went over and beyond to win an argument we had. He threatened to leave me and I told him I didn't need him to take care of Kerrigan. I could do it all alone. He was only bringing me down. I only showed at his family's house to say my goodbyes. I crushed his ego and the only way to repair it was to ruin me. I spent days in jail. I had never been in trouble with the law before and I cared for my daughter the way a mother should. I think Joe has some ties to the police somehow. I never had anybody on my side that could pull strings until now. Fey sneaks and lets me talk with Kerrigan on the phone. Fey, I owe my happiness and sanity all to you. I'm sorry you had to go through a similar ordeal. Nobody should have their freedom taken away from them when they are innocent. There was no evidence saying I had harmed my child. It's the worst feeling in the world."

She continued talking as she reached into her purse.

"I came to give you some documents you may need. Give these to your lawyer. It's the most used phone numbers from Joe's logs. I'm sure some of these relationships carried over from our relationship right into your marriage. I have found some of the numbers to belong to state workers, paralegals, nurses, mostly women. Joe is an opportunist and I'm sure he used these ladies in every way possible, even professionally. Please feel free to do with it as you please. One more thing, do you think Kerrigan may be ready to see me?"

Celeste speaks out of turn. "I will ask my husband, Fey's attorney, and see what he thinks." He can go over the documents Joe had drawn up and we can prepare a plan."

Fey speaks with full emotion and says "I would love that but Celeste is right. Let's do this the right way and you have my word on expediting the situation. I mean, who is to say a chance meeting at a park couldn't take place..."

Andrea is wearing a smile that could stretch over Peachtree Street.

"Goodbye ladies, thank you!" Andrea leaves wearing her smile.

We all say goodbye to this lovely lady. I can't imagine what she has gone through.

"Celeste!" Fey and I yell her name.

"What? We don't know her. We have to check out her story first!" she says defensively.

"She does make sense though. Who knows what Joe used to be tied into? How did she get the numbers? She said she didn't know anybody who could pull any strings."

Fey then informed us that it was her woman's intuition. Andrea printed them out from her phone carrier's website. She had been forced to become a spy just as Fey had. It was too bad she wasn't one step ahead that day at that family gathering. It would have saved her a lot of heartache. This intense lunch demands some retail therapy.

We hit the stores which prepared us for a spa day! We shared laughs and stories for hours. I would still get so tickled when Celeste would talk about Alec romantically. He's my brother and that's just not the way I saw him of course. He did remind me of Rich when it came to surprising Celeste with trips and gifts as Rich had done to my mother when we were growing up. They are the reason I believe in love so dearly. My mother, a passionate soul, rounded Rich out. Rich was very business oriented and driven. He moved here from Chicago and became one of the youngest lawyers at his firm to make partner. He was caring, compassionate and in his eyes, my mother was his gift. He knew she was the one from the moment she began to work for him. She guided him whenever he had become discouraged. They had disagreements of course but they always handled them and came out on top. Alec definitely followed by example. Alec was quite the ladies' man in college. He had tons of stories and little anecdotes or *"Alecdotes"* is what I liked to call them. He was *that* brother who always warned me about the guys I dated. I knew what they would do before they did it because I had a coach. Coach Alec made sure I was always current on the plays of the game.

Celeste took him by surprise. He didn't see her coming. He dated so much in high school and college because he thought he would have to settle for someone Rich approved of. Alec instantly loved Celeste's calm nature. He called her breathtaking, often. Later he would find out that this red head goddess came with an alternate voice as well. She was feisty when it came to things she was passionate about. She was a true redhead. He loved all the faces of Celeste. Celeste and Alec have been to Hawaii. I'm grateful to share my turn with Baby so that I can share my *"Anni*dotes" afterwards. I am refreshed after my spa day and now very well versed on Hawaii etiquette due to Celeste. I can't wait to see my Baby. Maybe this getaway will provide some room for growth. But my confidence in our love needed fertilizer to maintain well-being. Every moment we spent together would be just that fertilizer. Our time together was never forced. We just fell into it. I loved that side of him, that playful, carefree side that just seemed to push me over the top. I lived at the top when I was with him and I'm sure this trip would be certain of the same.

Chapter 6

Ma Ma said there would be days like this. "Anacelia, one day you will walk with peace," she said. Today was that day. My vision embraces the brown sugar sands and big rock candy simulations. My perception is that of a carefree little girl. My jewelry is made of flowers, my shoes of wet sand, my cup is made of a coconut and my being is made of sugar and spice and everything nice. I look over and stare into Baby's eyes. His eyes resemble a reflection of the water, the ocean's mirror. I am jealous of the sun because it is kissing his skin. I want to do just that but I can't move. I'm captured. The wind was whispering in my ear. I answered back with my breath. My breathing turned rhythmic, in tune with the damp air and sultry sand dancing with the wind. The trees were whistling, ocean humming... I was seeing sound. Baby reached over and touched my hand and my breathing started to sing a solo. He kissed my neck and my reluctant voice began to crescendo into moans. He was so close that the button from his opened, linen shirt was playing with my forearm. He began to strum my arm with his fingernails, tuning me up for his performance. Down strokes and upstrokes were alternated until my heart beat like the batter skin of a drum. The bass in his voice sounded in my ear and I straightened to an ovation, the finale of this Hawaiian concert. Encore, Mr. Davenport.

A scented breeze brushed across my face, awaking me. The smell was lifted from the chocolate scented orchids that decorated our room. The Chocolate Oncidium may be my favorite orchid due to the cocoa aroma. It reminded me of Baby's cocoa butter scent. Our suite smelled like a bakery. Chocolates laced with sea salt come to mind. Sherbet colored fabric kissed the four poster bed. The doors and furniture were draped in beautiful jewelry like fixtures that sparkled in the intimate lighting. This room had a relationship with love. The properly positioned chandelier over the bed could probably tell many stories. I look over at this man and my eyes start to roll, mouth waters. The possibility of a person's mouth- watering for another person is mind blowing. I now have visions of *blowing his mind*. His mind was located in the middle of his body, the real central nervous system. It controls all. His mind can read my mind. His mind sends signals to my hands… to my lips… I want to blow his mind. I take his mind in my hand and just like that I blew his mind under this stunning focal piece. It stares at us while we spend the morning narrating and directing under the sheets. This man plays his role very well. Under my direction, he produces a crave-worthy performance.

I don't know how I mustered up the energy to follow our event agenda. It was designed based on our likes and preferences. A brunch of granola, fruit, and homemade yogurt prepared us for a guided green house tour of an orchid nursery. Baby basically just followed me around. Every time I learned of a new orchid or smelled a new scent, whether cinnamon or lemon scent, he said I naturally gained a huge smile. He kept pointing out things just to make me smile. This being an apparent turn on for him, he kissed me in a different place every time I smiled. I was sure our antics would get us thrown off the tour. Playing a game of cat and mouse in the greenhouse worked up a hankering for snacks. My craving for him would have to wait. Some food would suffice... I passed on the Ahi jerky and avoided the spam and seaweed situation that Baby was indulging in... Macadamia nuts, papaya, and mango would prove worthy for our rain forest hike up next.

The weather was a perfect 80 degrees, accompanied by a light mist... We hiked through fences of bamboo and gazed at waterfalls and tropical scenery. I worked up such an appetite that we had dinner in our hiking gear.

Care free dining.

This island had an abundance of rice. It seemed it was served with many dishes. This catered to my palate, growing up with a Spanish mother. The pork themed dishes were plentiful as well. However, no Benadryl juice box for me tonight. I settled for a shellfish bowl which included: scallops, prawns, clams, lobster, and mushrooms in a Chile sauce. My salad consisting of baby lettuce, heirloom crab, octopus, caviar, and avocado preceded my amazing seafood symphony. Baby opted for crab chowder made from purple sweet potatoes followed by smoked swordfish, asparagus, and prosciutto wrapped mushrooms.

"Anacelia, we should have dessert in our suite." He motioned for the waiter to come over and I assumed whispered some details about dessert to him.

He arranged such a lovely setting. The balcony occupied fragrant Hawaiian Orchids, scented candles, candy and pastries. There was an aroma of kindness. Like redolent residuals of many nights, I could smell his will to please me. The sky was painted gold like the ornamented Rocher Ferrer chocolates that were sprinkled around the table. My favorite wine had become his favorite as well and we finished an entire bottle. His kisses began to taste like Moscato. He was literally sweet. He had become my definition of dessert. I wanted to indulge right there, but our semi private space could possibly be seen by others. I would be gambling with our affection possibly becoming a display. My conscience irked my physical need right into a moral spasm! This indecisive alter ego was interrupting me. I never felt so many emotions at once... I was fighting myself. My passion tempts fortune and I give in. I collapsed and positioned myself. Baby responded to the invitation. Our opposite positions caused an unspoken language to develop. We couldn't speak... Our emotions had our tongues... We only had body language. The night air was good to us and treated us like old friends. It welcomed us with open arms. We hugged back with our arms, then with our legs until our emotions spoke. My hell bent passion had guided me right to heaven and just like that, the language barrier between right and wrong was broken.

Waking up in this place was amazing. The panoramic view teamed up nicely with a couple's spa day out on the balcony. Baby asked the massage team to leave the tables so we could enjoy the view longer... The team obliged. However, we only made use of one of the tables. He rested his head in my lap, looking up at me. I noticed cloudiness in his eyes that I'd never noticed before. His eyes opaque charm, drawn out by the direct light, had never presented itself to me before this bright morning. Seeming so sensitive to sunlight, he buried his face into my abdomen. I felt something may be wrong but he looked up at me. He smiled and I engaged. All my thoughts were lost. I rested my hand inside of his robe. I could feel his heart beat with the backside of my hand. Similar to how a person would check for fever...

I am so overwhelmed with passion. This 9 hour flight home will knock me back into reality. I have to prepare for a few events. Who knew that in my lifetime I would be simultaneously living dreams? When I was a little girl, I wanted to work with children but I also took pride in creating things. I'm doing both. The universe also saw fit to place this outstanding specimen of a man in my life. The understanding and the giving of one relationship is a gift from above. Only few people share such a bond. I am one of those people. No matter what happens between us, I will always be grateful for being allowed to even experience such excitement. I can't look at him any longer. I am always drawn to him—a sexual magnet. I have to have him but there is no time before our sunrise volcano tour... Maybe just a few body kisses to prove my excitement before we set sea.

I adore him. I have to say to him, "As much money and power you have, you don't know what you're really worth. Do you? Do you know what kind of man you are? You're the kind of man women fight for—not fight over. There is a difference. Fighting over a man is just some basic display of not being able to control your emotions. However, fighting for a man means protecting his existence in your life. It's how I know Ivy will never let you go. She will fight for you. The idea of you is her way of life."

"Anni, Ivy...."

"SHHH!" I place my finger on his lips, softly so the gesture is respectful.

"Baby, you're the kind of man who makes a woman question what kind of woman she is. You're the kind of man whose energy demands questions. You're intriguing."

I'm drawn to touch that chiseled jaw line. I follow the lines of his face with my fingertips and hold his face with one hand. I place the other hand on his chest.

"Baby, you're the kind of a man whose heart beat responds to a woman's touch."

"Anni, my heart only responds to your touch."

He leans me down and runs his hand under my dress so that my heartbeat now responds to his touch. I gasp, my heart is thumping.

I'm lying on my side taking small sips of air every time he strokes me. He is now lying to the left of me... his left hand reaching over still flirting with my middle. My right hand is raised over my head. He clasps it with his right hand. Our bodies are facing each other. His feet are touching mine and I realize our bodies are forming a heart... The college girl in me surfaces and giggles with that college girl curiosity. I want to instantly know what my body will do from just touching. My left hand is free. I'm about to cross this heart. I reach over to his middle. Let's see if I can make his core dance. His abdomen is jumping, chest retracting and then his thigh muscles tighten. My right hand is still holding on to his, above my head, squeezing tighter and tighter every time he strokes my middle. I can feel his heartbeat in my left hand, though my hand is not touching his heart... Once again if this chandelier could speak, it would speak of the silence in the room being interrupted by moans and gasping. This man knew how to turn me on, get my motor running, and drive me crazy. I ran out of gas... I need to sleep this off but I can't. I gotta go meet the sunrise for a tour.

A boat tour does sound delightful. So, I continue out of bed in a *"gotta make the donuts"* stupor. I can't swim but I trust him to take care of me if anything were to happen. That's what soul mates are for. Baby wanted a helicopter ride but I felt a boat ride would be much more romantic. A helicopter sounds so... well... LOUD. My anxiety and my fear of the unknown are whispering amongst themselves. This man could talk me into anything... almost anything.

It's a picture perfect day. The flower in my hair and other adjunct accessories give the ugly life jacket some life of its own. *Drowning is not cute.*

Cute describes this man next to me. His demeanor was always subtle. The subtlety balanced out the intensity of his face. His lips were full of color. His eyes were of the ocean's hue and chiseled face was like island boulders. My mind was taking snapshots of Baby. He was becoming the sheer image of the memories I would have of my Hawaiian getaway. I've heard that the memory of something or someone is only that of images from the last time you remembered. I'm assuming this to mean that you're only having a memory of your last memory. This could be the explanation of how each time I thought of him was more vivid than the last. *Things that make you say hmmm...* If this only meant I would remember the same thing from this moment. That would be ok with me... Then, I notice the striking scene of lava sizzling into the ocean. I think my memory would claim this scene forever. I have to admit, the rushing waves and being close to this lava was stirring up a fright. The lava was pouring into the water. It was an intense experience. So intense that Baby's blue eyes now had red specks in them from the reflection of the oozing lava... Now, this... this would be my memory. What a way to close out this trip.

Chapter 7

"**M**rs. Hughes, it's so nice to see you again."

"Please call me Zora."

Waiter, two Amaretto Sours please. Annie, I hear so many amazing things of your work. How do you find time to make things beautiful and tackle a 9 to 5?"

"Zora, making things "beautiful" makes me happy. I also love my day job. I'm good at it. I'm fast with calculations and I can think on the fly, which helps in emergency medical situations. This same ability also allows me to remain calm in events with high stress levels, such as medical events or even a child's birthday party. When I was a child myself, it was notated that it was easy for me to use the left as well as the right side of my brain. I am both creative and rational. If your left side is dominant, you are said to be more logical while more creative as a "right sider". I have a chaotic rhythm, I suppose. As a teenager and young adult, I attempted many things. *A jack of all trades, master of none* didn't apply to me. I mastered everything I attempted. I finish what I start. Things come easy to me."

"Anni, I could have used your judgment back in college. I was driven but also very calculating. I only finished what I thought would benefit me... I never faced any consequence that came from my actions. I just dominated things. I was determined to stick with my plan to be a successful business woman. I had no time to be anyone's friend. My family barely saw me. I tried making room for love and being business minded, but I couldn't manage the two. I guess I'm a left-sider. I've been in love with my husband since college. He is just as driven, both Ivy Leaguers with MBA's. We fell hard in love and noticed our grades fell as well. We also noticed we were pregnant. Our parents surely would have cut us off had they known. We didn't tell them. I had an abortion by some woman I was referred to by a soror, a midwife. It was the worst experience I had ever had in my life. I remembered being severely dazed and cold beyond description. I left a little piece of me in that room that day. I was literally never the same. I can't have children now due to the botched procedure. I'm rich and successful. But the one thing I want I cannot purchase. I believe women should have rights and a say so to do as they please with their bodies. However, I tried to plan my own fate and I failed. Adoption may be my hope now. I devote a lot of time to pediatrics as well as surgical research, for reasons that were unknown to you before today. Thanks for allowing me to share with you."

"Zora, I am honored. You are an exquisite person. Your story is remarkable. I hope you find clarity. If you keep beating yourself up, you'll have to heal over and over. Find comfort in what you can provide for research. You and your story will make a difference. Things have changed. You and your husband have several avenues to take to become parents. First, begin with testing."

"Anacelia, we have come to accept that our act has determined our outcome of not being parents. I can't get pregnant again. We've tried. It's out of our control. You're an angel clearly because you believe in miracles. Hmm... That's it! Our theme for the event should be *Believe in Miracles*."

"Zora, you got it. You shall be my inspiration. Let's get down to business." I chimed. We discussed dates and ideas for hours. I think the meeting went well.

It's only been six weeks since we returned but six weeks of meetings, walk-thrus sampling food, creating skits and coordinating live music. I have a full plate, coordinating my brother's wedding and the, "*Believe in Miracles*" event for Zora. Both events will prove to be huge society markers. My Hawaii trip with Baby provided some much needed relaxation. But, I have now stepped back into the real world. I'm covered with invoices, props, and menus ...

"*Baby calling*" My phone rang startling me.

"Hi, Baby."

"Hey, gorgeous. What are you up to my dear?"

I'm designing. I'm slowly running out of room. My little Camry is becoming harder and harder to transport things in for meetings and such. I'm thinking of buying a bigger vehicle."

"I don't want you to be stressed. Is there anything I can help with?" Baby asks.

"Yes, Baby, just be you. I could never be stressed with you in my life and I love designing and creating. It's my safe place."

"Anacelia, you're my safe place. Anything that makes you happy makes me happy."

"Baby, I am happy. I will be just fine."

"Ok gorgeous, I'm a phone call away."

"Thanks, Baby, I have to get back to work… This benefit is creeping up on me. I have T's to dot and I's to cross."

"Gorgeous? Don't you mean T's to cross and I's to dot?"

"That's what I said Baby."

"Anacelia, are you ok? He confusedly asks.

"Yes, I'm just a little tired."

"You mustn't work so hard. Get some rest."

"Thanks for checking on me. I have to get back to work…"

- Banners
- Guest list
- Table linen
- Seating chart
- Centerpieces
- Programs
- Verify Menu
- Labels
- Signs and Posters
- Donation tree

I wake up looking at this list. I have fallen asleep working on it. Hours have faded away and I have been attacked with fatigue. I want to eat something but just the thought makes me sick. I can't bring myself to finish. The last six weeks have been very productive. My organizational skills have come full circle. This list however is draining me. I don't even want to look at it. I get up, hesitant to check my messages because I don't feel like returning any phone calls. A cold sweat comes over me and my stomach is in knots. My mouth waters and I know I need to throw up. I make it to the bathroom just to be interrupted by the doorbell. I let it ring and ring while I sit on the bathroom floor hugging the toilet. My phone starts to ring and I hear a knock on the bedroom window. I crawled over to the window and opened the drapes to see those beautiful blue eyes looking back at me. Noticing me on the floor, he demanded I open the window. Baby crawled in and held me.

"Anni, are you ok"?

I don't have the strength to laugh at the CPR quote.

"I don't know what's wrong. I just woke up ill."

"Let's get you back into bed. Do you want something to drink?"

"I will take some ice chips, please."

"Anni, I'll be right back."

"Baby, the crushed ice from the fridge dispenser will do just fine."

He rushes into the kitchen. The breeze from my opened window feels great. The weather is perfect for this cold sweat and insanity

VITA COOP

that's going on in my abdomen. Maybe it was something I ate. Through the drapes blowing in the wind, I notice a glimpse of red in my peripheral. I sit up and it's a huge red bow! *HELLS NO!* There is a brand new white Range Rover outside.

"BABY, did you drive this car here? Why is there a bow on top? Whose is it? Where did it come from?"

"Gorgeous, I see that your illness isn't affecting your ability to ask questions. It's yours."

"What do you mean? It's mine?"

"That's what I've been doing all day. When we spoke today you said you needed a bigger vehicle to accommodate your design business. So, I bought you one. I hope you like it. I wanted to surprise you. I didn't expect you to be crawling on the floor ill when I got here. I didn't mention it because I was immediately worried about you. I wish you would get up and go to the doctor my dear."

"Baby, I'm fine. I need to get up and go see this car. I can't believe you bought me a car. You didn't tell me because you thought I wouldn't approve and talk you out of it. But, I think it's a beautiful gesture... It's a very grand gesture. I don't know what to say."

"Anacelia, you don't have to say anything. It's my pleasure. It pleases me when you're pleased. I'm delighted to do things for you... to do things with you... I've been waiting on these moments. Are you up to going outside?"

"Yes!"

I throw some water on my face and dash outside.

"It's gorgeous!"

The color looks like a pearl. I open the car door to sit. The new car smell hits me in the face. It's delightful. The seats look like my brown sun kissed skin from my trip to Hawaii. Next to the paperwork, with my name on it, sits a familiar blue box. My eyes light up! It's holding a sapphire bracelet and earring ensemble. It's perfect! It will partner well with my gown for the benefit. This man knows just what to do. He's calming and drives me crazy at the same time.

"Anacelia, Have you eaten? Let me drive you to get some soup."

We drive off in my beautiful new car. He tries to run in the store to grab what I needed but I can make it in. I'd much rather accompany him inside than to remain in the car with my thoughts. We walk in and I feel the desire to snack. Grateful to have an appetite, we aim for the snack aisle. Standing in front of the chips, that I desperately wanted, was a little boy. I skipped right in front of him to grab my favorite salt n pepper chips. He poked me in the butt, asking, "Daddy, what does she have in there?" Baby couldn't contain his laughter. The boy's father quickly states that he recognized me from work and I once gave him stickers that were in my back pocket. Baby utters, "Good save" and pats the father on the back. I had brought a few pounds home with me from Hawaii. I clearly thought the five-year-old was referencing my huge butt. I was still a brick house with a garage but maybe now a double garage...

I gave the little boy a hug and promised to have stickers for him if he ever came to see me again. Maybe snacking wasn't a good idea, but I still wanted to eat. I grabbed chips and some sweet items. I wanted to cover all the bases. Baby grabs chicken noodle soup and Sunny Delight. He remembered my stories of my childhood favorites. He also remembered that I ate sweet and salty items when I was stressed.

"Anni, are you stressed about your upcoming event?

"I guess one could say I'm stressed. I just want to do a good job."

"You always do a good job. Let's go back to your place and de-stress."

We walk out into the parking lot and I'm looking for one of his cars. I forgot that we are in my brand new car...

Chapter 8

The fabric draped around the columns was a good idea. It was such an inviting scene. "Believe in Miracles" cascades on a custom backdrop. I placed a wish tree in the entrance. Donors can pull a wish from the tree and make it come true for the foundation. Each table is clothed with crisp linen and natural embellishments. Elements of water, earth and fire fill the space. I strategically placed the cards on the tables. The Davenports purchased two tables. The Townsends have a table that will be within eye distance of the Hughes. I think Rich and Neale will hit it off. These charity events are well known for networking. I hope Zora will be pleased with everything. She left most of the decisions up to me. She was the perfect client.

The servers looked stunning. The men are in black ties and women in black peplum dresses. I am in a coordinating peplum, long and blueberry in color, matching the blue orchids on the table. The sapphires Baby gave me are dazzling. The guests begin to arrive and I see Drei! He looks almost as handsome as my Baby.

"Anni, you are dazzling."

"Thank you Drei, I didn't know you would be here. You are pretty good on the eyes. Black tie affairs are becoming of you—especially when you're wearing a knockout red tie."

My word... entering behind him is Zieg and Nadine Davenport, Baby and Drei's parents. My voice has left me as I notice they are curious at our display of familiarity. They are unsure of who I am.

"Mom and Dad, this is Anacelia, Alec's twin sister."

"How do you do Mr. and Mrs. Davenport?

"Alec is Baby's oldest friend. We are pleased to meet you. Will your parents be attending as well?"

"Yes, Mr. Davenport, they will be in attendance tonight. I expect them shortly."

"Anacelia, you look stunning and what a beautiful name."

"Thank you Mrs. Davenport. You're beauty is eye catching."

"Please, Anacelia, call me Nadine. Zieg, to our table please."

"YES, Dear..."

The escorts will show you to your table... Zieg and Nadine Davenport.... That was a near heart attack moment—until I see Baby enter with Ivy. My knees buckle. Why would he bring her? Why didn't he tell me? Luckily Drei is still standing next to me. He extends his arm to escort me in saving me from this direct encounter. We walk in silence but I had to separate from him... I felt faint and had all the warning signals of a vomiting episode. I dashed to the ladies room. I made it before I ruined my gown... What am I to him?—just the other woman? How could he? *And the smirk on Ivy's face...*

"Anni! Anni! Open up", screams Fey.

"Sweetie, what's wrong? Drei said you're ill."

"Fey, I saw Baby with Ivy and I threw up."

The feeling that took over me made my knees buckle. The breath was taken from me. "Fey, how could he do this to me."

"He didn't even tell me she would be here. How the hell can I get through this? I feel terrible."

"Anni, I think we have bigger problems..."

"What? How?

"When was your last period?"

"For heaven's sake don't be silly I just had one before Hawaii."

"Anni, Hawaii was over six weeks ago, if I'm not mistaken.

"NO...NO... I'm just stressed. Help me get through this."

This was supposed to be an unforgettable night. The guest list was supposed to bring many prominent people together for a good cause. Instead the guest list had caused me so much pain. I must pull it together.

"Fey what ya got in that purse to pull me together?"

She hands me lip gloss and a chocolate bar... a breakup starter kit....

I must go and face Zora. I throw a mint in my mouth and put on a fake smile...

Drei is waiting outside the door.

"Drei please don't tell my family I was sick."

"No problem, dear. Baby is looking for you. He wants to explain."

"No need... I have an event to pull off."

HELLS NO... As if the night couldn't get any worse, Jax walks in from the side entrance, carrying a saxophone case, reading "Jaxophone". He must somehow be the house act. Great! Thank GOD he didn't notice me. Now, I have two men to avoid. Fey grabs my arm and we head to the Townsend table.... I need my family right now. My parents are sitting with Alec and Celeste. I sit at the table with my buzzer; my device to signal the hired hands of the event sequence.

Zora stands on stage wearing a flawless Vera Wang gown. Her speech is touching and also funny. She has captured the crowd... I signal for the band to get ready to play as she exits. I signal again for the dry ice scene to surround the opening act which was apparently Jax...

He begins a solo. The Saxophone has the guests under a spell. The atmosphere changes with lighting. Jax is playing *"Ribbon in the Sky"* which signals the ballet company to enter with sapphire colored ribbon wands. They dispense from four different corners and meet in the middle of the room. The tables are arranged outside of the dance floor on levels, so that each guest can witness the entrance of Asia, our star dancer. Asia enters wearing a white tutu laced with sequins, blue ballet shoes and a blue orchid blessed her hair. Jax is now singing while the band continues to play. His voice sounds as if Mahalia Jackson and Nat King Cole had a love child. Hearing his voice brings back so many memories. He was indeed the perfect man for this job. The universe had delivered once again.

Asia was 5 years old. Yet, she was already a remarkable performer.

Every eye in the place was on this beautiful little girl... Except for Baby's eyes... His eyes were on me. I'm sure he thought I planned for Jax to be here. At this point, I don't care what he thinks. I want this night to be about Asia and the children. She is a cancer survivor and she has filled this room with a joyful spirit. After twirling, leaping and bending, the male lead enters and lifts our little star into the air. She looks as if she is flying. He places her on a chair, on stage. At the end of Jax's song he walks over to Asia and says, "We believe in Miracles." Asia reaches up to Jax and places the orchid from her hair as a boutonniere on his jacket. Asia pulls her wig off and exposes her bald head. Her smile is so bright and there isn't a dry eye in the room. Asia takes a bow. The small curtain closes and no one is left sitting. The curtain reopens to the sight of this beautiful child. I toss a glitter dipped, red, rose out to Asia as the male lead escorts her. The guests take the roses I have placed on their tables and toss them at her as the male lead glides her back through the audience. I press my buzzer and the lights come on at the stage only where Zora is now standing. All eyes turn back to Zora.

"Ladies and Gentleman, please take this time to mingle, meet Asia and our children and get to know each other. Each of you are responsible for helping children like Asia. Give yourselves a round of applause. We thank you!"

I signal my buzzer once again. The lights come on and the servers began to dispense champagne and hors d'oeuvres.

Whew, I made it through the beginning. Zora makes it over to me. I extend my hand to her and she hugs me instead!

"Anni, I loved it."

"I'm glad you're pleased, Zora."

The band will play during this *"get to know you"* hour. Once a certain song plays, the guests will be asked to be seated for dinner. Then the *after dinner tribute begins.*

"Anni, it sounds like you have it all under control. And I do mean *ALL...* I noticed the attention given to you by a couple of fellows. You are indeed capable of handling stressful situations my dear. I am impressed. Carry on..."

Oh no, she noticed. I'm glad she thought innocently of it.

Baby finds me....

"Anni, you did an amazing job. I was surprised to see Jax here but he excelled as well."

"I was also surprised to see Jax. Furthermore, I was surprised to see Ivy here..."

"Anni, let me explain... I....."

"Baby girl!!" Rich interrupts.

"Rich, Ma Ma, did you enjoy?" I'm glad they saved me.

"You are talented beyond words, baby girl. "

"Ma Ma, I just pushed a few buttons."

"Princesita, it was beautiful. Is there more?"

"Si, Ma Ma, after dinner."

I didn't want to be rude so I acknowledge Baby's presence by saying, "You two remember Baby, Alec's right hand. His parents and wife are here as well. Baby, will you escort my parents to your table for an introduction?"

"Yes, of course." He knew exactly what I was doing.

"Follow me, Mr. and Mrs. Townsend."

I escape to the kitchen to check on the food preparation. Everything is on time. I sneak a couple of grapes but I'm still not feeling well. I see Jax and I suddenly feel worse.

"Doll, you and I could make a great team."

"Jax, I thought you were done with gigs and focused on teaching.

"Doll, this is my place. I own this event venue. When I saw your name as the planner, I volunteered to help with the cause."

"Jax, thank you dearly, you did an amazing job up there. It took me back."

HE GRABS MY HAND AND SAYS, "I wish you would take me back."

I pulled my hand back rapidly...

"Doll, I'm different. I've grown."

"Jax, I'm not a doll and I'm glad you're in a different place in life but I can't accompany you there! Now, will you please get ready for the next set? I buzz for the "kick off" song and one of the band mates makes the request that we sit for dinner. Dinner is served. The children's tables are covered with pizza and juice boxes. We also have a nurse on duty, my dear Fey. After all, we have precious cargo at these little tables. The kids are delighted.

I have planned for the second act to be a dessert show. My servers travel around each table with different desserts, ranging from Tiramisu to plain vanilla ice cream and pound cake, a southern favorite. Dessert is always easy to eat and the indulgence of the treats will pair well with the show. Let the show begin.

The servers are done. The curtain opens upon my signal. There appears a street light on stage. The sound of a bounced ball echoes through the surround sound system. A little boy enters the stage... He continues to dribble. He paces...

"I wish I could play basketball." He utters.

"You can." A man's voice enters (Jax)

The little boy turns to Jax and says, "Sir, I can't play basketball. I have cancer. It could hurt me if I play."

"What's your name, son?"

"My name is Jordan, after my dad's favorite NBA player."

"Jordan, you can do whatever you want."

"I want to dunk!"

Jax picks up the boy and holds him in the air. Racing to the rim, Jax screams, JORDAN DUNKS!"

"I can dunk! I can dunk! Thank you sir!"

Jax places Jordan down carefully and says "We believe in Miracles."

Jordan sits on the stage and Jax begins to sing *"I believe I can fly."*

A young choir enters, joining Jordan, all wearing basketball uniforms.

The song selection is perfect. The choir is made up of young boys and girls whom possess outstanding musical talents. Some who were told they would never sing or dance again. Some who have a love for sports or who are just happy to play outside. Jax did an awesome job with these kids. They brought the house down!

Standing ovation… The children are excited. I now know why I never needed to attend the practices. Jax had it all under control. Checks and business cards are being passed around. People's hearts and stomachs are full. The children are happy. Jax takes the time to tell me that these are his students! I could only smile. I am impressed at this well dressed triple threat standing in front of me. I am proud at the man he has become. This warrants a hug.

"Doll, you just made my night."

"Jax, I would be honored to work with you and the children. I never thanked you for the orchid you sent me. It was beautiful. It actually sparked the theme for tonight. You are the reason the blue orchids are among us.

"Doll, everything turned out great. I knew it would if you had anything to do with it. We work well together and to think you weren't even aware that you were working with me. I'm going to go see the children off. Please contact me soon."

"I will Jax. Thanks again."

VITA COOP

My face hurts from smiling. I am so proud of Jax. My part of
the festivities is over. It has now been passed to what I like to call
the "money team". They make sure the donations get accounted for.
Then the clean-up team comes in after guests are done. I've noticed
Ivy staring at me all night but I worked hard to ignore her to make
sure my job was done. But somehow now I am fixated on her behavior
toward me.

"Don't mind her, she's just counting my son's money," says Mrs.
Davenport *or Nadine as she has asked me to call her.*

"I beg your pardon, Nadine."

"That wife of his... We picked her but she's nothing like her parents. She was a dear child but she has grown to be quite a monster of
a gold digger. I guess people do change sometimes for the good and
sometimes for the bad (I immediately think of Jax). Zieg and I adored
her and Baby trusted our opinion. But our Drei, he's a different story.
As a matter of fact, I think he's smitten with your friend in the pink
dress, Fey? He has followed her all night. Zieg, let's go dear. Anni, it
was delightful to meet your parents. You clearly have been groomed
by greatness. I must go and say goodnight to my boys."

"Yes ma'am."

Mr. Davenport says goodbye with an endearing deep voice. He is
the silent, protective type. He is very protective of his fair skinned,
blue eyed wife. She takes her blonde hair down as they walk outside. The picture of his melanin blessed hand cradling her bare back

was memorable. As I watch them, I notice Baby putting Ivy in a car, sending her home. One question pops into my mind… "If they didn't sleep in the same bed, how did she hear him saying my name in his sleep?" I replayed our conversation back in my head and sure enough Ivy mentioned learning of me through Baby saying my name in his sleep. How did she hear it? I snapped out of it and hurried over to my family. "Celeste and Alec looked stunning in a matching tie and gown ensemble. Her champagne colored gown looked great with that red hair. Her green eyes match her emerald earrings and clutch. My family is beautiful. Baby is beautiful… I can't look at him any longer.

He comes over. "Anni, don't go."

"I have to Baby. I'm exhausted and I don't really have much to say to you."

I can tell that Ma Ma has overheard me—so I continue my good-byes to my family.

"May I take you home, Anacelia?'

"No, Fey will drive me."

"I think Fey would like to stay with Drei."

Fey interrupts, "No, Kerrigan and I will see Anni home."

Little Miss Kerrigan grabs my hand and skips out in her little pink dress that coordinates with Fey's. I love my friend. She is the epitome of truth and loyalty.

Mr. Hughes presents me with a check for my hard work. I notice

Jax and I wave goodbye to him. Baby stays behind and talks with Alec. I am positive Baby didn't realize he wouldn't see me again for months.

How will I ever be without him? I will have to teach myself how to live without him. Could I be pregnant?

Chapter 9

*M*y head was hanging off the bed. I was staring at the ceiling pondering about what the hell happened last night. He enters my view of sight. I see upside down flowers and Chinese take-out. He drops it all and kneels over me, facing the opposite direction. His lips were equal to my forehead. He kisses my forehead, my nose, and then my lips. He kisses my neck and breasts... His face is even with my abdomen which means he is now straddling my face.

I am panting, my heart is racing...

BEEP... BEEP... BEEP...

My alarm clock! I'm dreaming of him again. I guess I thought a nap would ease things but I wake up gazing in disbelief. I find myself outlining the trim of the mattress with my fingertips wishing he was here. I've never been in love like this. Letting him go was the hardest thing I've ever had to do. The silence in my bedroom is fighting with my thoughts and I miss his touch. I miss the way he inhales my presence when he is near me. How can I accept to never be able to receive that kind of passion ever again? It's proving to be catastrophic. Even my toes ache without this man. I could agree to continue to see him and participate in the lovemaking and the kisses that stop my thought process. I could think of nothing other than him touching all over me while in the bed together. But I just couldn't go on like this.

We are linked together through my family and I know the time will come when I will have to see him. I will be next to him and how will I ever get through this.

I can't believe I haven't seen him in so long. I think of him all the time. Every hour occupies some memory of him. He calls... he emails... but I don't respond. Jax's actions are similar but not as striking as my Baby.

Baby's calls are more frequent and detailed. Both men are on a mission. One man is trying to convince me that he has changed, and the other is trying to convince me that he has not changed. I don't want to hear from anyone right now. I am so weak with indecisiveness. Besides, I don't think Jax would be on cloud nine about me being pregnant with another man's child.

Celeste calls and I have ignored everyone for long enough. I feel compelled to talk with her.

"Anni, how are you?"

"Celeste, it's tough but I think I will be ok."

"Anni, Jax has called me. He is concerned about you."

Celeste, Jax was a good friend to me and was easy to talk to, the definite runner up in this contest. My romance with Baby may have coerced a possible relationship with Jax.

"Anni, I don't understand."

"Baby is my ideal man. He spoiled me with the perfect kisses and the amazing sex. But what spoiled me the most was just him, his presence. I am addicted to the man's shoulders! His build, his makeup, his vibe captured me. He is a real life remote control. I see him and am instantly turned on. I feel spoiled just to know him. Our worst day together would be better than most people's best day together. The world was designed for two people. I believe we come in pairs. We are born with GOD given gifts, each other. We have to obey and that gift will be awarded to us. When Baby was awarded to me, I didn't obey. I was running off with Jax. Now my gift is now wrapped in a different package, a married package. Why else would GOD design him for me and then not allow me to have him?

I feel accomplished just to know my soul mate. How many people can say that? Even if I wasn't in love with him, I would still love him as a friend. I have accepted that Baby is my gift and no one else will compare. Therefore, it makes it easier to accept another man because I lost my gift. So I will have to take the consolation prize."

"Anni, are you saying you're going to be with Jax?"

"No, I'm saying Jax is the next best thing. I don't know what I'm going to do. Maybe it's a precocious conclusion."

"Anni, I am here for anything you need. I will protect you, I will cover for you. I will put the wedding on hold and dedicate my time to helping you get through this. "What do you need?"

"Celeste, I just need time. I'll be just fine. Thank you for always being there."

"ANGEL! ANGEL!" I could hear Alec calling her in the background.

He called her angel due to her name being a derivative of the word celestial —heavenly. He found peace in it.

"Ok, Anni. Alec is anxious. He has been so worried about you. We will check back in. Please call Fey. She is also worried. We love you."

"I will. Love ya back!"

Celeste was indeed an angel. She had always been there for me and was severely protective. She adopted this form of living after being sexually assaulted at an early age. She was at a friend's slumber party when the older brother of her friend interrupted her sleep with sexual advances. She was only eleven years old. Life had coerced her into becoming a shield to others. She was always on alert. He promised her chaos if she told anyone about what he had done. He threatened her family and she never told her parents. She, however, made a vow to herself to ruin him. He lived a life of crime and uncertainty which made it easy to destroy him without contaminating her family. With her legal ties, Celeste would make sure he would never see the outside of a jail. She had a calculating brain housed in that cute little red head of hers. She wasn't one to cross. She was quiet *and* dangerous. Alec found this endearing—an angel with proverbial horns. He would never leave her side as it would endanger her trust. He was dedicated to her and so was I. I loved her dearly. She and Fey have been my dearest friends for ages. I must call Fey and tell her I'm functioning.

Fey answers on the first ring. "Anni, are you ok?" I thought I was ok. But a cloud of mixed emotion started to rain down on me and I instantly cried. I usually laughed whenever Baby asked me the same thing. The CPR dialect was cute and enchanting. Now, it was just painful.

"No, I guess I'm not ok." I'm wet with tears.

"Would you like me to come over?"

"No, I'll get over whatever this is."

"Anni, most of what you're feeling is confusion. You never gave him a chance to explain. You need to know why he brought her to the charity event. Call him."

"I don't need to know. It's simple. He brought her because she is his wife. I can't call him. I can't even carry on my daily duties. Breathing is hard. I'm functioning on the lowest form of life support, which is ice cream and chocolate. Life is just an image right now. I know I'll get over it but I just want to be alone and think."

"Anni, I will respect your process but please call if you need anything."

"Thanks, Fey. I'll see you at work."

"There will be a surprise waiting for you at work."

Oh great. I'm not up for surprises, I thought to myself.

I want to be alone but this silence is loud as hell! Maybe work will be the best thing for me. Driving the Camry allows me to feel like my old self; the *pre Baby Anni.* I couldn't drive the Range Rover. It haunted me like a big, white horse powered ghost. I have to give this car back to him. The gifts... It just doesn't seem right to keep them. It doesn't seem right to keep the baby... What have I done?

Dropping my name tag under my desk proves to be the highlight of my day, as I found an unopened bag of leftover chocolate from Valentine's Day under there. Still a bitter sweet moment as I love chocolate but they were given to me by Baby. I thought work would ease my mind, but staring at the flowers and cards from both Baby and Jax are clouding my judgment as well as my eyesight. Fey could have told me that my surprise was a jungle of flowers. Through the jungle of roses, orchids and sunflowers, I finally find my phone to check my voicemail. I have several messages and I stumble upon one from Zora. She wants to meet with me for lunch. I am delighted. She could provide some clarity for me at this point. I'll call her.

"Hi, Zora. How are you?"

"Anni, I'm great. Thanks for calling me back promptly. I have a business opportunity for you. Will you meet me for lunch?"

"Absolutely, is the Thai place ok?"

"Yes, I'll meet you there at noon."

I'm concerned of her detecting my eagerness. I needed to forget about these persuasive men in my life. I was excited to learn what Zora had in store for me. The hours could not have gone by any slower. I went to the restaurant thirty minutes early. Zora arrived in a stunning business suit and here I am in scrubs. She still, however, managed to lend me a compliment in my underwhelming attire.

"Anni, you're glowing. Could it be one of those men from the event that's responsible for this glow?"

"Yes, one in particular." *Tears flowing...*

"Anni, I'm sorry. I didn't mean to trigger anything. Are you ok?"

"Zora, I *am* sorry. I didn't mean to cry. My hormones are ruling my life right now."

"Anni, are you saying what I think you're saying?"

"YES! I'm not sure why this is coming out so smoothly to you. I haven't even told my family or my best friends."

"Anni, your words are flowing because it's usually easier to tell someone that is not affected by your news. I won't judge you. We all have weak moments."

I totally forgot about what she wanted to meet me for. I've been ranting about Baby. This took up the duration of my lunch break.

"Zora, I feel awful. What did you need to speak to me about?"

"It's not important. We'll pick up later. You go back to work and call me afterwards. I would like to sit with you some more."

"Sure Zora. I would like that."

Again, time alone in this car is making me feel claustrophobic. I'm closed in, fighting with my anxiety and am about to lose the fight. My depression is jealous and is trying to step its game up. I run in to work and had to sit in the bathroom after my legs gave out. My palms are filled with tears. I sat on the floor watching my tears hit the tiled floor.

"GOD, please grant me a remedy. I am uncertain of this feeling in my gut. The fear of the unknown is driving me insane. I love this baby so much. His baby… This baby deserves better. I need to go home. I can't work like this."

All I want to do is sleep and my phone keeps ringing. It's Zora. I better answer.

"Hi, Zora,"

"Anni, are you ok? *This again…*

"No, not really. I apologize for not calling you. I left work early to come home and gather my thoughts."

"No worries, dear. I called to simply check on you. You didn't seem well when I left you and I just wanted to talk with you. I once made an emotional decision that changed my life drastically. I don't see any conviction toward a decision. But, I don't want you to make the same mistake. You seem distant and disconnected, nothing like my first meeting with you. Please be certain of any decision you make. Perhaps it may help to discuss your situation with a professional background to help sort things out. You can't go through this alone. Neale and I will help you every step of the way."

"Thank you, Zora. This is all so very sweet of you. You are a compassionate person. I haven't made a concrete decision. I have, however, decided against an abortion. The baby will be given up for adoption if I don't decide to keep it."

"Anni, do you care to share the details with me? I may be able to help you?

Does the father know?"

"The father does not know of the pregnancy. He is married and I have decided not to tell him. He is in a political debacle; a marriage. He seems stuck in it. He wants out but maintains the fiasco. I have gotten myself caught up in it. I love him dearly and I know he loves me. I can hear his heart beat double time whenever I touch him. . But somehow, I feel he will always support the decision he made to become married, even if it was a business arrangement."

"Anni, I may have a remedy to your situation. Neale and I can adopt your baby. But we want you to be sure as I want to continue a business relationship with you as well. This way the baby will still be in your life. It would benefit Neale and I to seek counseling about this. You should as well. We all want to be of sound judgment."

"Anni, are you still there? Anni?"

"Yes... yes... I'm still here. I'm touched by your proposal. You would be great parents. I need to think about it. You may have shed some much needed light on a very dark and grim situation. Thank you so much. I'll be in touch."

"Anni, no matter what, I'm here for you. Please think this through."

"Indeed I will."

"Goodbye, Anni."

I have to make a doctor's appointment. This has to be done before I can make any concrete decisions. Maybe the Hughes can go with me and possibly to a counseling session. We can sign a confidentiality agreement and none of my friends and family will ever need to know. I will tell them I decided to become a surrogate as they will all be around to watch my growing belly become a display. They won't understand but will accept my decision because they love me. If I tell them, they will only try to talk me out of it. I can't be a single mother and purposely bastardize my child. Zora and Neale may be the best thing for this unborn miracle.

I will throw myself into planning Alec's and Celeste's wedding. The baby will be born around that time. When they are on their honey moon, I will be giving birth during the Holiday season. When Celeste decided to have a holiday wedding, she didn't see this little gift coming. She only wanted to go skiing on her honeymoon. I'm sure Joe will be getting out of jail around that time and the protective order would have been lifted by then. I can only imagine the emotions Fey will go through when he is back in the general population. The wedding will have a great *pick me up* effect on everyone. I will call Zora in the morning. I am mentally bankrupt at this point. I have nothing left.

I wish I could call Ma Ma and Rich. My mother has such a calming nature. But I don't want her to know what I've done. She won't judge me but I'm sure she would question the change in my character. She was once scorned, by my biological father. He left her pregnant and confused. Rich rescued her. Maybe Jax was my rescuer. *I doubt it...* Jax was my best friend. We entered what should have been a forbidden zone but we will always be friends because we have a reciprocal understanding of each other. Jax is a lot like me and I always knew I wanted a husband like Rich, a structured man, someone to even me out. Jax wasn't really that person but I guess people can change. *I doubt it...* I'm full of doubt, not like myself at all. I am afraid that my parents will be concerned of who I've become because they know me not to be this person. Oh what love is capable of!!

For some reason, my mind travels back to Saturday morning clean up sessions with Rich; *Al Green* playing in the background. I hear, *"love will make you do right... love will make you do wrong... make you come home early... make you stay out all night long..."* As a kid I didn't know what kind of truth this man was spitting out through those soulful vocals. Now I understand. Love is sometimes unspeakable but at times it's loud. Love is darkness and light. Love will make you quiet but will also make you speak loudly. Sometimes your words can't be found but love makes your heart speak. It makes you drive across town just to get a kiss. It makes you spend money on flowers that will eventually die just to capture the moment of a smile. Love makes you stay in the bed all day and learn each other. Love makes you... the list is endless. Sadly, love makes you become pregnant by a married man...

Rich is a soulful man. I loved being raised in the house with him. He listened to all kinds of music; mostly blue eyed soul like Linda Lyndell, KC and the Sunshine Band, Michael McDonald. But when we needed to fall into the groove of things, we listened to Sly and the Family Stone, Stevie Wonder, The Isley Brothers, Al Green, The O'Jays, and Frankie Beverly. My mom would sprinkle a little Sade, Billy Ocean, Enrique Iglesias, Gloria Estefan, Paula Abdul and Miami Sound Machine into the mix. Freddie Jackson and Luther Vandross took me through a rough spot for sure!

Jax and I definitely vibed when it came to music. But, he's a rhythm and blues kind of person. I listen to anyone who moves me... Eric Roberson, Jill Scott, Common, Outkast, George Tandy, Marsha Ambrosius, Maxwell, Anthony Hamilton... I see music as poetic lyrics. If it grabs me, I commit to the artist. My love for music came from my parents. Blue eyed soul grabbed me at an early age. Leigh Jones, Pink, Adele, Joss Stone, Daley, Robin Thicke... Rich deposited that blue eyed soul right into my lifestyle. It is the quintessence of how people judge a book by its cover. People are so amazed when a white person sings soulfully that they gave it a name, *"blue eyed soul..."* Who knew I would have an actual blue eyed soul enter my life on a level I didn't even understand? I see those blue eyes in my sleep.

Right now I'm depending on Lauryn Hill to get me through this heaviness. She will go everywhere with me in the form of ear-buds, headphones and speakers! I think I'll invite Sade, Adele, Mary, KeKe and Alicia to the pity party as well. Alicia to the pity party as well. Get ready girls! This is gonna be a tough ride! Where is my Butter Pecan?

Listening to music makes me ask should I have casted him out of my life cold turkey? I had willingly given away my orgasm. I gave up the love and the passion. That touch alone would carry me through tough times. Now being without him was making me experience withdrawal. No touch, no kiss... When will the feeling in the pit of my stomach be lifted? The feeling below my stomach was even more demanding. I miss Baby.

Chapter 10

"**M**s. Townsend. Ms. Townsend." My name echoes in my head, as I realize the nurse is calling me back to be seen. It's sonogram day. Zora and Neale want to adopt a boy but will take a girl of course. They are a beautiful couple and they should be meeting me here soon. My doctor knows of the arrangement. When I give birth, the Hughes, Zora and Neale, will obtain all rights. I'm sitting in a room that will prove somewhat similar to the room I will give birth in, minus the view. I'm sure there will be no windows in the delivery room. The window here is clothed by mauve drapes and the view is masked by rain. I walk over to look out and see the Hughes pull up in a stunning charcoal Jaguar XRJ. Zora is draped in a mesmerizing cobalt wrap dress that hangs from her matching raincoat. Neale is dressed in a suit that coordinates with the car. Zora adjusts his tie while he holds the umbrella over their heads. They pass the sign that reads Alpharetta Medical Professionals and continue in. I walk back to my bed to have a seat and wait for the tailor made Hughes to walk in... A text message alert comes through from "Baby", an ironically fitting name in this situation, but this is actually a name he is recognized by. He earned his name from being the last born. I call him Baby for his boyish good looks and his beautiful baby blue eyes. He's the only black man I've ever met with blue eyes. His skin owns possession of a caramel tone. Ocular Albinism, Waardenburg Syndrome, a recessive gene could explain the reason for this blue eyed soul on the other end of this text message. I can't respond to this genetic mystery right now. I reach to read his text...

"Hello gorgeous." The screen displays.

I sigh with great depression as I grimace. If he only knew what I was doing... If he only knew I was pregnant with his child. I drop the phone as the door to my room opens... A tall, short haired woman walks in and places her cobalt coat down and greets me.

"Hello, gorgeous" She now says.

I hide a subtle smirk at the coincidence but I reciprocate with a similar greeting. "You're quite stunning yourself, Mrs. Hughes." Her husband shadowing behind her, extends his hand inviting me to shake it. I oblige with a firm handshake. The businessman in him is pleased. As this is a business transaction. I nod to acknowledge and we immediately fall into an unspoken vernacular. The doctor enters and speaks with a welcoming bedside manner. "How are you folks?" We all provide a good southern smile and answer differently; an orchestra of the words "fine"' "ok" and "great" roll from our tongues simultaneously. The elephant in the room silently introduces itself at this exact moment and the awkwardness is interrupted by a suggestive beep from a machine.

The doctor utters, "Shall we begin?"

I try to relax as the tension between Zora and Neale can be cut open with one of the scalpels I noticed when I walked into this sterile environment. The doctor narrates the procedure while I stare at the ceiling. He announces that the overall health of the fetus is in good standing. I allow the sonogram picture to be passed to the Hughes. I smile through the pain.

I'm glad that's over. It was way too intimate in that room. Two strangers watching someone poke and probe me. I'm not too fond of the experience.

"Goodbye everyone." I race out with a "til next time" tone in my salutation. Never looking behind me, I head to the elevator on my journey home. My white Range Rover waits for me in the parking lot, the gift from Baby that I only drove because I was reluctant in putting gas in my Camry. The Range was supposed to replace my Camry. But the very specific teachings, passed down from my mother, taught me to never replace a practical item that I owned with a frivolous gift from another. My Toyota is parked in the garage of my three bed/two bath home. Both purchases fit nicely into my surgical tech budget. A job that plants the seeds for the career I was blossoming; event and home design. I work. I save. I build.

The cool marble floor welcomed me into the lobby as I stepped out of the elevator. This car ride home will grant me time to accept what just happened back there. "The Miseducation of Lauryn Hill" is playing in my headphones. Lauryn accompanies me a lot. We ride out. I settle into an easy space.

The new hospital just opened. The orange cones and signs near the beautiful glass entrance grabbed my attention. I didn't notice the piercing blue lights behind me. I pull over as the sirens suggest.

"Ma'am, are you familiar with the Move Over law in Georgia?"

"No, officer, I am not."

"Ma'am, you are to merge to the left lane when you see an emergency vehicle off road. You failed to do so... License and registration please."

I gasp at the news of this law and my obliviousness. I hand him my license and registration. He walks back to the blue light show behind me.

He returns asking if I have insurance.

"Of course officer. Here is my insurance card."

"Ma'am, you're tag reports your insurance as being invalid. This card you presented states otherwise so I'm going to have to impound your car due to the discrepancy. Can you call someone to pick you up?"

"Officer, I can call my carrier and validate my coverage."

"Ma'am, I don't have time for that. You can clear it up with the judge. The only phone call I need you to make is to call someone to pick you up. The wrecker will be here in 20 minutes. Please leave the key in the ignition when you exit the vehicle."

As I process what this belligerent, mustached man has ordered, I begin to dial the only person who would rush to me in 20 minutes. The phone rings for what seems like a lifetime.

"Gorgeous?"

"Baby, I need you to send a car for me."

" Yes, of course. Send the address."

"Thanks Baby."

And it was just that simple. Baby was on his way. No questions asked. He would do anything I needed or wanted. He was going to be next to me again. I'll be sitting in his car inhaling his scent. I'm more worried about being around him than I am worried about my vehicle.

Arriving promptly, Baby opens the car door and searches for me as he exchanges an indescribable look with the officer. It was a look of familiarity, hard laced with a "how dare you" snarl. The officer speaks immediately and they share an inaudible conversation. I wanted to hear the conversation but I was still sitting in my car. My car is left on the side of the road, with the key in the ignition, as the aviator wearing officer who looks oddly familiar, has instructed me to do. As I walk up to Baby I catch the tail end of the conversation.

"Judge, I didn't know. Please don't take my badge."

Baby hushed this gentleman into a very quiet state. The officer was such an overbearing jerk before. It's amazing what kind of emotion the threat of your livelihood will evoke. But, he had no problem endangering my livelihood before the judge was on site.

Baby welcomes me by embracing my face with only one hand because he is holding my citation in the other. He then places his hand at the small of my back coercing my movement toward his car. This display of affection warns the officer's common sense. He now assumes the basis of how I know the judge. Baby was the youngest judge in the area and had a reputation for being fair. He believed in teaching in the courtroom. Catering to the community was his weakness. He was my weakness. I'm sitting next to him in the car and immediately ache for him.

"Anni, are you Ok? This prompts a smile from me as I always reference a CPR dummy when he asks me this question.

"Yes, Baby. I'm Ok.",

"Anni, why didn't you explain your circumstances over the phone?"

"I didn't want your ego to brew on the way here."

He blurts, "Driver, roll up the partition, please." The driver may be secluded but there are still three occupants in the backseat; myself, Baby and my conscience. The guilt surfaces as I think of how *"Mrs. Judge"* has contacted me to meet her and divulge all of our details of my relationship with him. But his embrace snatches my attention back! "If you call Anni, I'll come running." My conscience disappears as he kisses me.

We manifest all the signs of a true romance. A ribbon of air is shared between the two of us as passing lights strobe around our closed eyes. Our eyelids are glued shut with content. Determined to visualize nothing more than his touch, I forget we are confined to a car. Thoughts flow. The chemistry is hot enough to fog up the windows. The same fog clouds my thoughts and I don't realize the car has stopped. I open the door in an attempt to get out of the car. The light from the interior awakens me more. I can see his eyes. Those eyes! That mouth is addictive. It automatically draws another kiss. His kiss has always been a drug. There's nothing left to do but obey the urge. The need is keen. Whose kiss is supposed to do this? Whose touch is supposed to summon this kind of reaction? It has to be a gift put in place only for me. Feeling the need to un-wrap my gift and indulge more, I decide to exit because the desire is venomous. I now understand that only his touch can sometimes feel like venom; signaling every part of my body to shut down and be on alert. Exhausted from my mind and body fighting, I exit the car with dizziness.

Baby follows.

"Anni, stay with me. I miss you."

I stumble backwards, intoxicated by his words. I utter, "Baby, I can't. I just can't. Please give me some time."

"Anni, I don't understand."

"Baby, please. I need to put these emotions to bed."

"At least a hug, gorgeous?'

I hold out my arms.

While hugging me, he whispers, "I love you." I can't speak. I smile awkwardly and walk into my home without looking back.

Surprisingly, I make it to the couch without dropping. The words

"I love you" ring in my ear. I would like to reciprocate but I can't admit it to him.

Aware that I might at times seem awkward to him, I try and hold those words in. But, they become bitter in my mouth. I feel if I could just spit them out they will taste sweet. They will shoot out eventually like that of icing in a piping tube. Song lyrics race in my head. "His kisses taste like Amaretto..." "He is the sweetest thing..." "Kiss on the collar bone..." He resembles a sugar rush given by a slice of cake drenched with honey. I swear he needs theme music... something clever... something moist worthy. He's sexier than the healing of Marvin Gaye. He's something to make Suge Avery sing about. *The Color Purple* reference stirs up the laughter within me and allows me to gift my face with a smile. My Baby is a walking bakery... like something good to eat. Just the thought of him transports me to the sweetest places.

My mind drifts and my state geared from dazed to mesmerized. My mood is that of an old cafe with music playing in the background... patrons entering the door... A breeze comes through. If you're standing outside, you get a faint smell of vanilla blowing in the wind. Caressing all senses at once; the touch, the smell, and the feel of being high... A rhythm but also the blues...

He's like the piece of cake before dinner that your mother said you can't have. However, you reach for it anyway because no one is around to slap the back of your hand.

My day dream is interrupted by my phone ringing. I send it to voicemail. I can't speak to him right now but I can't sit here without knowing what he is thinking. So, I check the voicemail.

"Anacelia, please call me. I'll make the arrangements for your car."

Oh no, he is calling me by my real name. He only does this when he wants to remind me of how we met and how we are meant to be. "Anacelia" is of Spanish origin, meaning "unknown". A pun created by my Spanish mother who was pregnant by a Trinidadian whom abandoned her. She could never embrace what could possibly come of this union. So, I was born, Anacelia--the unknown. It is said that people with this name tend to be natural leaders. They are self-sufficient and ambitious. Generally, they want to make their own decisions in life and are not afraid to take charge or manage a situation. It is important for them to avoid extremes of bossiness or shyness. They tend to be impulsive. Professionally, they can be successful in political leadership. My mother found comfort in this name as she was the maid of a single white politician, Richard Townsend, a Chicago native. I'm glad she later became his wife. He adopted us and gave us his name. We were born Alec and Anacelia Townsend. That twin brother of mine means the world to me. It was a surprise to my mom and Rich. They didn't expect twins. Rich displayed unconditional love for both of us. Alec of course followed in his footsteps as a lawyer. Alec being Baby's colleague and best friend, both had been groomed by their dad's to be great and so they were. Baby thinks he and I are meant to be. I am his politically incorrect soul mate as I have settled into my choice of a medical background instead.

We hid behind the politics as we cradled our artsy sides. He is a beautiful artist and sculptor. He has provided so much of my inspiration as a designer. Designing Alec's and Celeste's wedding should be challenging. I'm sure Baby and wife will be in attendance. He seems to have to hold her on his arm for purposes unknown to me. He and I will have to see each other due to our families and friends being in sync. This will be the hardest time of my life. My family is calling continuously. Messages from Fey and Celeste have taken over my voicemail. Alec is even calling me more than usual.

Baby called and I didn't answer, which prompted him to email. He wanted to meet badly.

"Anacelia, I have something important to share with you." PLEASE MEET WITH ME."

I agree to meet him for lunch and our conversation quickly went to Zora's event.

"Baby, I thought you were ashamed of what we had done. Ivy was draped over your arm like a living tennis bracelet. I was terrified and felt abandoned. I've been dealing with a tremendous heavy heart. I couldn't eat... no sleep.

Baby, Ivy came to see me... at my home before our New York trip."

"What? Anacelia? Why didn't you say anything?"

"I didn't want to cause any chaos. I just wanted to go to New York.

When I saw you together, it was the first time I felt like the other woman."

"Gorgeous, she will never be you. You were meant to be my wife. I filed for a divorce…"

I began to sob uncontrollably—so much that I didn't notice Alec and Celeste sitting at a nearby table. Fey was now standing next to Baby, smiling. A waiter presents me with a covered platter. Hidden balloons are released, violin sounds are coming from construction workers. My lunch hour has turned into a flash mob proposal. I'm so surprised that I never realized Rich was my waiter. Baby had asked him for my hand in marriage. Suddenly, Ma Ma approaches wearing a look of approval. Baby removes the box from the platter that is the shade of his eyes and asks me to marry him. The air gets thicker, my breaths get shorter and the tears are heavier. I drop down, two knees to his one and he realizes my tears are mixed with joy and pain.

"Anacelia, be my wife and whatever is frightening you will vanish."

"Baby, yes I want nothing more than to be your wife."

"So, gorgeous, will you… will you say yes?"

"Yes, We say yes……………"

"SHE SAID YES! SHE SAID….. Wait, you said we… We? Anacelia?"

"Baby, I'm pregnant."

A silent chorus of shock and surprise spread over this mob like a cloud. My family was shocked into silence. Strangers gasped and began to applaud. My Baby helped me up and placed his hand over my stomach."

"Anacelia," he had no words. He just placed the ring on my finger and held me. I couldn't look at Ma Ma. I had kept a secret from all of them. Baby was happy but I didn't have time to think about my family and how they are taking it. I slowly opened my eyes to assess their reaction. They were all smiling. What a remarkable day! Now, to tell him I had put his child up for adoption.

Dear GOD... I'm a Devil.

Chapter 11

You never know what the day will hold... I was in the process of accepting that my life with Baby would not be possible. Now, I'm staring at him on my couch scrolling on his phone. He keeps sneaking kisses from me. He can't help himself. Damn, these kisses make me smile. I feel under a spell of some kind. I even get high from his memory.

"Baby, what are you doing?" He puts the phone down and kisses me...

"Research," He says.

This man is so inviting. He gets down on the floor facing me while I'm sitting on the couch. He continuously kisses my abdomen.

"I want to make you happy." He says in-between kisses.

I want to make him happy but I don't know how he will feel when I tell him of the agreement with the Hughes. My emotions are fighting right now as he places his head in my lap. I'm glad his head is turned so he can't see the mischief in my eyes. I will have to speak with Zora first thing in the morning. I'm terrified of crushing her dreams. I can't believe I had been so captured by my unanswered questions that I arranged to give our baby away. Love is an unpredictable thing. Through the thought of losing this man, I had planned an adoption. I don't know if I ever would have gone through with it. I would love this baby as I had loved him. It was a part of me. I think Zora knew that my emotions had come to a standstill. I had been free of emotion during my agreement with her and Neale. How could I bring two more people into this?

Baby raises his eyes to mine, "Gorgeous, stay by my side. Don't do that to me again. Always talk to me regardless of how you feel. Don't leave me."

"I'll never leave." I promised.

Somehow, I think, being in a fake marriage has made this man capable of loving more. He is so passionate... passionate enough to be sitting on the floor rubbing my feet at the moment... passionate enough to begin to kiss my thighs. He has been without passion and now wants to experience it in every way possible. His heart comes with instructions and I shall oblige him. His fingers are crawling up my leg. I know where this is going and I am along for the ride. I will follow this man anywhere.

"Baby, please tell me how you arranged it all... the proposal."

"Gorgeous, it started after the charity event. I stayed behind to speak with your parents. Alec helped tremendously. I didn't expect you to stop speaking to me. I never knew Ivy's presence would hurt you so. She was only there to make her last appearance as my wife."

And there it is... the reason she was around was to prove she wouldn't be around in the future. She didn't want to divorce but had no choice. Her love for things would eventually keep her going. She had been a nuisance to his happiness.

I should have given him a chance to explain. Hormones mixed with shame made a dangerous recipe for pain. Pain allowed me to sit at home and think of how I *lost* the one person who understood me when I had actually pushed him away. The one person who finishes my sentences, the one person who shares my creative drive... The one person who was designed for me... I let him go before and repetition was becoming the blueprint for my love life. This time I am going to step out on faith and conquer my fears. I am going to become Mrs. Zieg Davenport. Well, the second Mrs. Zieg Davenport... I can deal with that.

If I focused on being the second wife, I would be running a race that could never be won. I will never be first, no matter how hard I cheat. I would have to accept the defeat. So, in my mind I will create a diversion, a coercion to make *her* seem flawed. I will automatically seem greater by default. My inner mean girl hates her. I mustn't. But it doesn't seem fair... Oh what do I care? You can only render competition with two things that are the same in some way. Therefore, there is no premise to compete. She and I are so different. Her skin is not like mine. Her thought process is left and mine is right. She zigs and I zag. Therefore, I don't feel the need to feed this desire to conquer. I'm too far gone to understand why he chose her. She is just a memory and I shall live in the present.

Chapter 12

Am I really hearing birds chirp or am I stuck in some fairy tale? It's morning and the smell of food is delightful. The birds are having a choir rehearsal outside my window. I could definitely get used to waking up to homemade waffles every morning. My Baby was gifting me with breakfast before I had to go off into the world and tell one of his biggest supporters I could not give her my baby. Zora was indeed a fan of Baby and I wondered if she knew he was the father. She is very observant and I know she probably had a clue or two based on behaviors from the charity event.

"Gorgeous, do you want to take your breakfast with you?"

"Yes, I do need to make a stop before work." I gulped.

"Will you grab the paper before you head off? Baby asked.

I head out to grab the paper for this monument of a man standing in my kitchen eating waffles and my phone rings!

"Hello."

"I woke up to an empty bed as I do most mornings. My husband never shared a bed with me. But, there is something pulling at my soul more knowing that he is waking up with you. You have ruined my life and I will seek revenge."

The call is interrupted by a dial tone.

"Ivy! Baby you have to handle this. Take care of her. She can't just call and threaten me!"

"Gorgeous, don't stress. It's not good for the baby. I will handle Ivy. She is all bark and no bite. I will make sure she never does this again."

Oh this man… he embraces me but this time it doesn't draw out the negative. I forget about his hug and begin to embrace the thought of Ivy finding out about my baby. She will lose all control! Baby never gave her a chance to flaunt a pregnancy for the public eye. Ivy will see RED!

"Anni, listen. You have nothing to fear. Please go to work and I will handle this. You have my word."

"I'm depending on you. Will you be here when I get home?"

"Yes, gorgeous, I wouldn't be any other place."

"Ok. I'll call you soon."

Today will be an unforgettable day! Ivy is stalking me and I have to tell Zora about my decision and hope the news never gets to Baby. I walk in to work and overhear Fey on the phone. I can tell she is talking to Drei. I am so glad they hit it off. She needs this right now. Fey slides away from her desk, a giggly fog leads her off to speak with him privately. I can't help but notice something she has been working on nestled under some care plans. I have to sneak a peek!

DIVORCE IS FINAL

I wake up to my clean floor—free of his socks

My entrance to the bathroom is clutter free

The toilet seat is down.

My monthly visit to the E.R. has disappeared

No more bruises...

I haven't seen a cast in a while

My hair has grown healthy and strong

My nose is free of blood

My lips don't kiss the floor anymore

No carpet burns

Make up is a choice and not a requirement

I can read a book

I can look someone in the eyes

I'm a woman again

I can breathe without my ribs hurting

My silence was killing me

I found my voice

I hope the next woman listens.

I suddenly have no words. I blessed the piece with a tear. I try to hurry it back under the care plans so she wouldn't notice but the damned thing is stuck to my maple syrup fingers. I shouldn't have been trying to stuff that waffle in my mouth while I was driving.

"Anni, have you been crying?" Fey is good at calling me out on things.

"No, I'm fine."

"Oh I thought my poem made you cry..."

Busted!

"I had to read it. You've always been a good poet. I'm glad you're teaching Kerrigan how to expand her thoughts to paper as well."

"It's therapeutic and helps me point out the good things in life. Now let's put it away before the creator comes by."

We called our manager, the creator, because she thought she was GOD. She would also create problems just so she could fix them and seem important. She once mixed peanuts in her candy jar so a co-worker wouldn't ask for her food. The coworker was allergic to nuts! Luckily the coworker was obedient and didn't help herself. She could have died from Anaphylactic Shock! The creator was nuts herself! I once saw her pull a paper Christmas tree from a box and display it. She later told one of the patients that she had made it *with her own two hands.* I don't know how she ever got the job. She was unskilled and clueless. She made things up as she went. She probably knew some-body who knew somebody who slept with somebody. She was a toxic, passive aggressive nightmare. I witnessed her go to a fast food place to have the poor drive-thru worker fired. The young girl forgot to give the creator a straw. She argued that drinking without a straw would make her sensitive teeth hurt and that the girl should be fired. Then she patted the girl on the back and said, "*I'm doing this for your own good.*"

Fey and I always got a kick out of describing her antics to Celeste. We called these little antics "creations". These creations were sometimes plentiful but it depended on whether or not she took her happy pills with a glass of wine. She was a pale skinned demon. I called her the Albino Wino. At the moment, she was counting paperclips to see if anyone had taken any. Today should be a good show. Her theatrics would last me until lunch. Then, my meeting with Zora.

Chapter 13

The look of this Thai food is not so comforting today. I can't tell if the physical or the mental part of this pregnancy is challenging my appetite. Oh what Zora will think of me? I cringe thinking about what I need to do as I see her walk in.. She's smiling so big. She is wearing one of the smiles that can't be erased. I put this smile on her face and now I'm about to take it away. What kind of person am I?

"Anni!! I'm so glad you phoned me... I have wonderful news... life changing news."

"Zora, I need to tell you something. Let me go first. I've been thinking..."

"Anni, I'm pregnant!!!!!!!" Zora interrupts.

My water glass hit the floor. My tray of food followed. As Zora kneels to tend to my mess, she continues talking from the floor. She is looking up at me and telling her miracle pregnancy story. I am dumbfounded!! God does work mysteriously.

"Anni, I really listened to what you had to say. Neale and I went through several doctors. We always assumed the problem was with me. After being told the abortion had been the deciding factor of us not getting pregnant, we mentally gave up. We never had Neale tested! If not for you, we probably would have never done it. I owe you my life. Now on terms of adopting your unborn, we would still love to help you as much as possible. Does the offer still stand? Anni dear... speak. Are you ok? Anni, are you ok?"

An impulsive smile widens on my face. My comical reaction to this question was back!

"Yes, Zora, I'm ok... There is something I need to share with you (even though I'm off the hook, I feel the need to tell her). The father of my child is Judge Davenport."

"You dear girl, I'm aware."

"Zora, you knew all along?"

"I only knew after the charity event. He kept his eye on you the entire night. Anni, I got where I am by being observant but also by being quiet about things I shouldn't know. It's a gift." I offered the adoption as my way of helping you to get out of a sticky situation. I respect Judge Davenport but you have become like my little sister. I adore you and want nothing but the best for you. I saw you hurting and didn't want you to make a hasty decision as I had done in my past."

"Zora, that's not the end of it. We're going to be married."

"Anni, I am aware of this also."

"Zora, how? How could you? Judge Davenport wanted to make this a smooth transition for you. Think about it... The restaurant of which he chose to propose was my establishment. He never loved Ivy. We were all excited to see him get a chance at happiness. You also deserve that happiness. I am concerned that all of this happened too fast.

But you two have history and I think you should continue to build. Design a life together and don't allow life to get in the way of living. Now, that being said, I do wonder about this second gentleman from the charity event. Is he of any concern?"

"No. He is indeed someone from my past that found his way back into my life. I was preoccupied with him during the time I initially became acquainted with Baby. Jax kept me busy. It was the backpacking, skiing and snorkeling from all the trips Jax and I had taken that side tracked me from Baby. But I've thought of Baby since the day Alec introduced him to me. Jax is a good person but he allowed his love of the fast life and fast women to taint his decision making. Besides, you can't help who you love. I will explain everything to Jax. His friendship means a lot to me."

Cringing, I think of the real reasons on those trips with Jax that ripped me from him. Jax's life was involved… mostly in the wrong things.

"Anni, life has delivered some very special gifts to you. Accept them, embrace them, and live! You will be a great wife and mother. I'm certain of it."

"Zora, you will be great!" Let me help in any way I can.

"Anni, I'm over 40 and pregnant. I'm going to need all of the help I can get. There are precautions I have to take. But we are up for the challenge. This blessing has been in the works for a long time. Neale has been stuck, poked and probed to get to the bottom of our failed attempts at pregnancy. We finally conquered it. I am grateful to you. Now, you get back to work! Continue with your day. You and I are family now and we can talk and share our pregnancy experiences together." "One more thing Anni..." She continued. "This man has been through a lot to be with you. Please understand that he loves you. But also understand that the happiness that you were granted was taken from another. There is one person out there who will not benefit from this. Ivy! She is vindictive and her soul doesn't exist. She has really changed over the years. Some people ripen with age. Ivy seemed to bitter. Be careful of that one. I'm sure you can handle her but I'm worried about the safety of your baby. A scorned woman is one to be mindful of."

I immediately think of the phone call I received from Ivy this morning. Zora is a seasoned woman and she knows her stuff. I am very mindful of this time bomb I have come to know as Ivy." I give hugs and kisses to my mentor and the new godparent of my child. Back to work I go. Fey will love this...

On my way home from work, I stop by the farmer's market. I think today warrants a special meal for Baby and I. I send him a text. "What would you like for dinner?" His reply of "you" knocked me off my feet. This pregnancy bomb turned him on even more I think. He was a man in love and I was in love with him. We spent every off day together. He camped with me until things could be resolved with Ivy and the estate. We shopped for baby items together. He has even insisted that we purchase a house. I agreed but I will also keep my house *(my mama didn't raise no fool)*. I will eventually settle into my role as Mrs. Davenport. But right now I must focus on being Mrs. Wedding Coordinator… Celeste had her claws into me day and night. The "bridezilla" term was nothing compared to this Bridal gangster. The Kodak moments were turning into Prozac moments!

It was going to be her special day and I will pull this off. Baby was also counting my every step. He thought planning the wedding may be too stressful on the pregnancy. I'm a Townsend but by blood I'm a Lopez. The women in my mom's family pumped miracles through our veins. My Ma Ma was right by my side. She had become my assistant as well as Fey. I have Fey on *vow* duty. Celeste and Alec were not the, "write your own vows" kind of couple. I commissioned Fey as well as Baby to create a piece of Art for a wedding gift.

Months of food and cake tasting fueled my will to plan this wedding. Nothing like a little sugar rush to get a girl through. Shoving cake into Celeste's mouth got her to shut up for at least a little while. She finally decided on an amaretto based cake with a hazelnut filling, an excellent choice. Baby Davenport was happy about the other desserts that would dress the table. My baby was flipping inside over the Red Velvet cakes, miniature pecan pies, sweet potato cupcakes and a host of other holiday favorites. They would have a huge role in the theme and play the hosts of the party in my tummy. I loved the tasting ceremonies. I couldn't drink wine so… Let's eat cake!

Maybe I had been overdoing the eating. My abdominal muscles were caving it seemed. The cramps were indescribable. Months of prepping, lifting, passing, pushing, and designing were catching up with me. Before I knew it I was sitting in a bag of silk fabric. Sitting turned into sleeping. Baby woke me up and made me go to bed. I couldn't sleep in the bed. My back was at odds with this body pillow that was given to me at the baby shower. Fey and Celeste insisted and Zora hosted it. I knew I would get a lot of things I needed and also a lot of things I didn't. This damned body pillow was something I didn't need. I wanted to throw it off the top of a Peachtree Tower! These cramps and I are going to go sit in a rocking chair. Sleeping sitting up eased the discomfort. When I woke up Baby was lying at my feet, sleeping on the body pillow. This man...

Something just didn't feel right. When I stood up I felt immediate pain.

"Baby wake up and call Fey."

"I should call a doctor shouldn't I?" He quickly answered.

"No Baby please call Fey. She will know what this feels like. She has miscarried before."

"Anni, are you saying you may be miscarrying?"

"Baby, please call Fey. I think it may just be Braxton-Hicks contractions. You can usually feel them after 20 weeks of pregnancy and we are well passed that now. Just call her please."

"Ok gorgeous..."

Fey agrees with me and we decide I should stick to bed rest for a while. Fey and Ma Ma can handle Celeste's rants for now.

Celeste calls and of course apologizes for working me so hard. It's time for some girl time anyway. They came over and it was like old times...before Baby times... Before Joe times and before the wedding of the decade began to take place. Joe was going to be released soon and Fey was not looking forward to it. He didn't know how to find her. But he had come to hate her and he has always hated us. He tried to strip her of everything good in her life. Kerrigan had been visiting her mom and was still writing poetry like Fey, a characteristic that Joe once described as useless and worthless. Funny, these are the words that come to mind when I think of him.

Baby had court earlier so the girls are going to take me to my doctor's visit and then ice cream which has replaced the wine drinking. My doctor was a friend of Zora, and I always received a cup of fresh strawberries and a massage at the visits... The waiting list for this practice was longer than the arm of justice! But every once in a while a little name dropping doesn't hurt. Zora ran this city and we helped her. My circle is that of strength and bonding. Together we had ties in the medical, judicial, beauty, food and entertainment circles. We were all in a good place. Zora also used this practice for her high risk pregnancy. We always synced our visits so we could hang out. Ma Ma and Mrs. Davenport are going to meet us all later for ice cream. The thought of all the women in my life gathering for me was pleasing. It's good to be loved. Drei was in town for business and it was going to be a task keeping Fey dedicated to this evening. Piedmont Park may never see her today. She was dying to get to him and I understood. I gave her my blessing to disperse. She left so fast, I thought she had evaporated. Love is a powerful drug.

A movie in the park sounded delightful! I'm sure the men are getting together for a poker game and a cigar smoking contest or something. My Baby always made time to sneak in a text message. The most recent read "I can't believe you're mine."

My reply... "Believe it".

I, however, got a strange text from Fey. Drei had stopped her by the guy's little gathering to say Hi. She overheard a conversation about someone getting out of jail and how they were preparing for him. She said you couldn't lift the testosterone with a forklift. Who could they have been speaking of? With all of the Legal Beagles in the room, the topic of discussion could range from blue collar to a blue body. They came into contact with people from all walks of life. I was just curious about who was walking out of jail early and why it was so important to them. Probably just a *one up* contest. I can only imagine The Davenport men, the Townsend men and the new sidekick, Neale, working on a legal collaboration. I'm sure Zora has trained Neale well. He was no stranger to success. He will round out the circle nicely. These men were distinct in looks as well. Any woman who walked in would gasp for sure. Mr. Davenport was an early model of

Drei and Baby. My brother was easy on the eyes as well... As much as a sister could notice, and Neale could stop traffic with his smile. Rich had gold wavy hair and was one of the wittiest men I knew. It was a room mixed of race and power. They were not to be reckoned with.

As much as I loved them all, I hoped they would all be cleared out when I got home. A great day out demands a great night of pleasure... my kind of bed rest. I am gonna practice some Kegel exercises with my partner... (I hear a choir singing in my head.) This man does it for me. Nobody feels like he does. If I could have somehow put in a special order for a man to be sent to me, he would be it. Signed, sealed, and delivered with a bow wrapped around his........... ankle.

My mind takes me to odd places when thinking of this man. Strangely, it also takes me to even places. He's my balance.

Chapter 14

I never much liked shopping for Christmas trees and shopping for one at the top of the season was frustrating. I always felt that the magic was in the tree decorations. It was the fall and I had to assume the tree farm would produce a perfect tree for Alec and Celeste. It would have to be tall enough for the entrance of the reception. It was my idea to stage a Christmas tree for the guests to place their wedding gifts under. I mean it *"tis the season."* I wanted to deliver a winter wonderland for Celeste. Our little flower girl, Kerrigan would be a snow princess. I have decided to have her toss manufactured snow instead of flowers. An evening wedding will create wonders for the ambiance. The bridesmaids will hold lighted candles instead of bouquets. Celeste will get the trendy wedding she requested.

The days before the wedding are becoming shorter and shorter and my belly is growing and growing. I'm so glad I don't have to wear a bridesmaid's gown. But I still need to go for fittings to make sure my gown can wrap around Baby Davenport. A simple empire waist gown should suffice but with eye catching coordinates. Stopping in for a fitting will be a good idea while already out shopping for a tree. I'll stop in alone. The girls would just spend the time trying to convince me that I'm not going to grow anymore. My belly reached the door before

I could. The lovely attendants rushed to the door to help me in. I do love the sight of beautiful things and this dress boutique is making my eyes dance. Then, I see the sight of a familiar blonde head. Ivy! *She happens to be in the store on the day of my fitting?* What are the odds?

"Anacelia, are you enjoying your life? My life!"

"Ivy, how did you know I would be here?"

"I didn't. Our circles are overlapping."

"Ivy, I'm no fool. This area is far too eclectic and artsy for you. You don't have a creative bone in your body unless you're creating drama which is exactly what you're doing. But, Baby can fix this with a simple phone call. You're lucky that I'm pregnant or I would fix it right here... right now..."

I completely turned around to address her and she gasped for air when she saw the pregnancy. I thought for sure she had found out about it already. She grabbed her chest and fell to a seat. I didn't have to say another word. I went to the back and continued my fitting, just after I called Baby to inform him of Ivy's new attempt to hijack my happiness. I'm sure she was somewhere upfront simmering. Baby was already on his way to put the flame out. Oddly, I glance at a huge black truck outside that really resembles Joe's truck. I know my mind is fried now. I'm seeing things.

Baby is here to offer some clarity. I grab my dress and Baby spits the words out "Ivy leave her alone. I'm going to place a protective order and then you'll have to deal with me."

"I'm not going to let you get away with this. You wouldn't give me a baby and now... now her!"

I can't leave without saying something to this idiot..." Ivy you're trying to drown a fish. Your words can't harm me... Your presence means nothing to me. I will continue my life as you should continue yours. You were a business deal. I'm his life long vacation. Move on. Let's go Baby."

"You won't get away with this." Ivy rushes through the store in a rant.

'I don't know why she was here, Anacelia, but I'm sure it was just a coincidence."

"Baby, it doesn't even matter at this point. She can't change a thing. The world won't change for her. Last time I checked, the world was still round. Once she realizes that she will move on to the next business deal. Imagine if Fey and Celeste would have come with me. Things would have really taken a wrong turn."

"I'm absolutely certain of that. Maybe you shouldn't share this with them." He suggests.

The look on my face is priceless. "You're kidding, right? I can't wait to tell them. This will call for an emergency girl's meeting."

"Okay, gorgeous, as you wish. Have your fun with it. You can always find joy in a mess. I love you for that. I love you for everything that you are. This life is going to be so different than what I am used to. I hope I can be all you need me to be."

"Baby, you are like a comma. Without you some things just

wouldn't make sense. I need you in my life. You have completed this little fragment of my life." You are who I am supposed to be with. Now let's get Celeste and Alec married. So we can be next."

"Gorgeous, that's the best thing I've heard all day. Let's go to a nice restaurant and feed Baby Davenport."

"The down lighting in the restaurant is amazing. It is creating art like shadows on the tablecloths. I will have to take this into consideration for the wedding since we timed it for evening. Lighting makes all the difference in a romantic setting. The wedding is set for an evening wonderland. I can't wait!

"Anni, what's on your mind? You've been staring at the light for minutes now."

"Baby, my attention was on the wedding again."

He reaches across the table and it sends a shock through me. I still react when he is about to touch me. It's an amazing feeling. I need to focus on him… on us…

"Gorgeous, the wedding will turn out great. I'm sure you're under a little stress because it is your brother and your best friend. In the words of Drei, you got this!"

"Baby", I can't wait to see Drei. It's such a treat that he and Fey are hitting it off. Joe was a tremendous burden and Drei creates such a different scene for her."

"Anacelia, listen?" *Oh no, my real name followed by listen is never good…*

"Joe finished his program…"

"He's getting out?" I grimace.

He's already out." He admits.

"Baby, I have to tell Fey."

"We didn't want her to know yet as we weren't sure of his release date. But he got out this morning."

"We?"

"Yes, Drei and Alec know as well. Drei is going to take care of her. We definitely didn't want you to be concerned during the pregnancy."

"Drei will tell her tonight. He will not leave her. He is in the process of repositioning things to contribute to her life more. He may be moving here sooner than we thought."

"Waiter! More water please for the lady."

"Baby, I don't need water. I need wine! Now unless you can turn water into wine, Jesus… Get that waiter back here." I demanded.

"Anacelia, you know I can't allow you to have wine."

"Well fine… order me the biggest slice of chocolate cake, chocolate ice cream and a chocolate milk shake. I might as well overdose on chocolate. I'm going to the bathroom."

I didn't think my day could hold any more surprises! Jax is here. I clearly need to deviate from my frequent spots. These people are appearing like optical illusions. I only know they are real when the theatrics begin! First Ivy, now this.

"Doll, Is that? Are you…?"

"Yes, Jax. I'm pregnant."

"Is this why you haven't returned any of my calls?"

"Jax, it's been really complicated. You weren't left out of the equation purposely. You will always be my friend but I didn't know how to tell you since you have been so upfront with your feelings lately. I didn't want to hurt you."

"I noticed your ring? May I ask?" He asked under his breath.

"My fiancé is here waiting at the table. Would you like an introduction?"

"Doll, I can't. Maybe at a later date… I'm afraid I am just too taken at the moment. I would hate to come off in a negative manner."

He grabs my hand and he is shaking. "Goodbye, Doll."

"Goodbye, Jax." I solemnly whispered.

And just like that I think my friendship has ended. He sounded so final. I couldn't even look back at him… I couldn't look back at the man who had tried his hand at a relationship with me before Baby. Sadly, Baby always had the winning hand.

Baby will be wondering what's taking me so long. I get back to the table and my chocolate cake is waiting. "Waiter, bring another slice?"

"Gorgeous, that's not good for you. Are you sure you want to indulge in that amount of sugar. Will you rest well?"

"I won't rest well without it, Baby. Now, order me a cake for home, please." I want to go home, bury this day in this cake and get some sleep."

"She's pregnant and didn't tell me. I thought our friendship meant more! Who does she think she is? All the good times we had traveling. She was always with me during my performances. My mother warned me that this would happen. I should have listened to her. I must stop this. She can't marry him. I won't allow it."

"Jax... is that you? JAXON IS THAT YOU?" I scream out!"

"She thinks she's going to just take my husband. I worked hard to obtain that position and she just walks in and takes over with her antics of love. I will not let this happen. She will marry him over my dead body!"

"Ivy! Is that Ivy I'm hearing! IVY, WHAT DO YOU WANT?" I scream out again.

"Anni! Wake up! Wake up! You're talking in your sleep! You're calling out for Jax and Ivy in your sleep." Baby interrupts my nightmare.

"Baby, I could hear their voices vividly! Now they are invading my sleep. It's only guilt. I meant to hurt no one. It's discouraging to have to hurt people in order to love you."

"Come here, gorgeous." Baby cradles me.

Just like that his arms made this crazy dream seem so small. It was hard to know that other people are hurting while I'm enjoying this man's simple touch. I can only imagine losing him. I often wonder if Jax feels the same way of me. If he does he must feel like he is losing a part of himself. I remember how I felt when I thought I lost Baby for the second time. I was stuck in a dark place. I'm holding on this time.

"Gorgeous, do you have some sort of concern of Jax that I'm not aware of? I know Ivy's visit wound you up today. But what's this about Jax?"

"Jax was at the restaurant today. It was the first he learned of the pregnancy. He was weird and shaky about it. I'm even sure he was crying when he walked away."

"Gorgeous, Jax lost his chance with you. Relationships and marriage are decisions. However, love is not. If you can actually be in a relationship with someone you love, it's considered a prize. He wants to claim his prize now and I can't say that I blame him. You are an amazing woman. Even I couldn't live without you. You are loved by two men and…

"Baby, do you hear that?" I abruptly interrupted.

"It's just the rain, Anni. It's coming down heavily."

"No… No… It's not! Listen. It's tapping…"

"I run over to the crying window, sad from the rain. But the image outside was even sadder. It was Jax! He was standing in the rain right outside my window. I run outside, grabbing a little yellow umbrella that Kerrigan had once left behind.

"Anni, where are you going?" Baby questioned.

"Baby I have to talk to him."

"Jax! Why are you here? It's 3 a.m.!" I screamed as a couple of drops of water ran into my mouth.

"Doll, I messed up! I'm sorry I messed up. That should be my baby you're carrying. If you feel like you have to be with him, you don't! I know I wasn't ready before. I'm ready now and I will take care of you and the baby. I can't be without you. All that time I'm sure you felt like I took you for granted. The truth is you were the only constant in my life. I was consumed with the idea of becoming a better man for you. I didn't know I was pushing you away. You and I have history."

He continued talking at a fast pace, blurting out each word as I tried to understand if he was speaking Hebrew or English. My mind was in a whirlwind.

"Doll, back then, my thought process was tangled in my web of a childhood. The person I thought was indestructible, my father figure, had been destructed, destroyed in a mindless altercation. This unknown presence interrupted my thoughts. I later learned it to be the fear of the unknown. My karate instructor no longer had a heartbeat. For what I had come to know, the heart of my biological didn't beat... At least it didn't beat for me... It had been taken over by a different substance. It only went pitter pat for a high. That high had beaten my childhood senseless until it finally regained consciousness when my karate instructor resuscitated it. I think he saved my childhood's life. I wish I could have saved his. I live in that childhood. I can't remember my first steps or the first spoonful of baby food that I spit out, but I can remember looking through the bars of my crib, watching my Pop's fists go up into the air and then disappear into my mom's face. The memory is so clear to me. I've always been afraid of becoming that person, of becoming him. So, I buried myself into traveling and music. I made countless efforts to mentally be with you. But I couldn't. I didn't think I was ready to ever be faced with such emotion. I didn't know how I would react physically. I have realized that I am not my Pops. Each time you kissed me felt the same but different as if each time was new. God clearly appointed you to be my muse... I can only create when I am alone or when I'm with you... No one else brings this out of me. It's easier to be with you. I can now admit to how I feel and my words are flowing better. These words are dripping from my mouth, in a race with the rain drops that are falling on my face." He's now stumbling over his words in his excitement to get them out...

Jax continued amid the rain and the tears falling down his face...

"Doll, I love your personality. You are someone who needs to be in my life every day. You used to be with me every day. Now that this is gone, I can't function. The way you love music drives me. You're the only person in my life that shares this with me. I love music and I love you. That empty feeling without you is not welcomed in the pit of my stomach. Only you can make it go away. When I saw you again in the farmers market, all of the memories started to rain on me again. It hit me like a storm and the overcast has followed me thereafter. My days are dreary. My mind is cloudy... I remember so many things about you, things that I can't find in anyone else. I remember that the entire inside of your thigh is a birthmark that looks like the map of Mexico. I always joked that my favorite place to explore was Mexico. Do you know how I miss going to Mexico?"

He touched my face and I'm sure Baby has noticed through the window.

"Jax, you are used to me. I'm familiar to you. You and I have a strong bond but it's a different bond. Let's go inside out of the rain."

"No. I don't want to go inside. Please hear me out. Doll, he married someone else over you. I would never have done that. I waited to get my life together and I'm sorry that I thought you should wait for me. I need you in my life."

"Jax, our life together was planned around secrets, your secrets. We were traveling on a bogus mission. You know you were involved into things. You sold me a dream. It never lasted long enough to maintain the happiness. So, I returned home. But, I'm not going anywhere. We will always be friends, but never compare yourself to him. You are two different people. There is no comparison to be made. You are one of my best friends and now I'm going to lose you because you have been kidnapped by emotion. Where is the Jax I know?" I desperately asked.

"That's what I've been telling you. The Jax you knew died overseas. That life is over. You were all I thought about. My hunger for women has been fed by you. Each day, I craved you more and more. I only have an appetite for you. That secret life is over. I made some terrible decisions in hopes to find what I was good at. I have since dedicated my life to being a better man. My tour only made me realize that life is short. The suspense and power from making those exchanges was all smoke and mirrors. I was terrified of the life I had made for myself. I always had to watch my back and sleep with one eye open. I finally dominated that part of me that wanted to be a drug smuggler. I ceased all activity. All I had was my saxophone and the thought of you. I was pretentious and selfish to assume you would wait for me to get my shit together, but I have to try."

"Jax, the life with you was exciting but not in a good way. I was also terrified. I was there for you out of loyalty. I helped you to make sure you would never get caught. You literally threw me into becoming the brains of the operation. I had no choice. I have to live with what I have done, with what we have done. I carried your ego all over the Western United States. You trapped me Jax... Baby is good for me."

Jax interrupts. "This man got you pregnant and then wanted to marry you. Doll, that's a trap if I ever heard one."

"Jax, you have it all wrong. He didn't know I was pregnant when he proposed."

"Doll, you're telling me that this man with so much money and power wasn't capable of finding out that you were pregnant. He was so driven by power and what people thought of him in the past that he married his first wife for status. Do you not think that he would marry you to avoid scandal and blame it all on love?"

"I indeed love her." Baby breaks into our conversation. Clearly he ran down, after seeing Jax touch my face, wearing nothing but jealousy and his pajama bottoms. I never even heard him creep up behind me.

I hope that is all that he heard. If he found out what I had done in my past... I wondered to myself.

Baby continues with his defensive tone. "You're out of line here. There is no need to plant ideas in her head. Nothing will form from this. She knows how I feel about her. I understand that you are hurt but you are about to lose all respect here showing up at this hour and throwing accusations."

"Judge, I'm not here to gain your respect. I'm here to make sure she knows the truth."

"Jax, thanks but no thanks. I can handle myself. Go home, out of the rain. We will talk later." I begged him.

"But Doll!"

"JAX GO!" I blasted him with every emotion as my fuel. I hated thinking of those past times.

Jax finally leaves me to process all of this. That yellow umbrella was useless. The memory of that happy face painted on it would haunt me forever. It was not a happy moment. I had been so full of the moment that I tossed it. I ran back in, Baby following me. I entered the bathroom, closing the door on Baby. I am soaked. We are both soaked but he will need to go use the upper level bathroom. I need to be alone for a minute.

"Anni, are you ok?" He was knocking softly on the door!

"Baby, not now! I just want to take a shower."

"Can I take a shower with you?" He pleaded.

I open the door. Saying no to this man has to get easier. Right now I can't do it.

He peels the wet clothes off me and holds my belly.

"Gorgeous. I…"

"Baby, please no words."

He kisses me and kisses my belly. Baby Davenport is responding to all the theatrics for the evening. I'm tired and all I can think about is sleeping. The shower was soothing and the caressing at the hand of Baby was just what I needed. He washed my hair and washed the suds off my body. He kneeled to wash my legs, right down to my toes while I used the bath seat to sit down. My skin felt like silk and was so sensitive to touch, only his touch. Poor Jax didn't stand a chance. Baby must've known my mind was wondering back off to the incident that happened just only a few minutes ago. At that very moment he sent a current up my leg with an unexpected kiss on the top of my foot. He grabs both of my knees and relaxes them on the shower seat. Washing my legs and thighs, he rinses each place with a kiss. My baby bump is cradled in my lap and is catching the stream of water from the above shower head. The top of Baby's head is catching the remainder of the water as he kisses me higher and higher up my inner thigh. Baby has now found his way to Mexico. That first kiss to Mexico sends my head back into the tile. He reaches up and cradles the back of my head but without ever moving his lips. I couldn't care less about a little head tap right now. I'm more concerned about my bottom lip because I'm biting it so hard. Jax who?

Chapter 15

The months have wasted down and my waist size is going up. The dressmaker has made an adjustable gown for me and she is a designing genius. The months of planning are now over. I finally get to see it all come together. I hope my brother is pleased. The tree looked amazing when I left last night. The designs in winter white, gray, and rose gold, all capture the essence of Augustness. The chairs are in fitted chair covers with rose gold and copper tones on the surrounding twigs and lights.

I'm assuming the guys will all be on time and not held up due to some lingering issue from the bachelor party last night. After a long night of a pampering party for Celeste that was interrupted by an exotic dancer, we've been caught up all morning preparing for Boudoir pictures. I love evening weddings. They allow plenty of time to forget about the night before and coast into the festivities. Fey is here with a snack of headache pills to be chased down with Mimosas. However, I have also arranged servers to serve us ladies as we hang out with the hair stylists and makeup artists. We will catch all the random shots we need for her memory book. The guys have a separate photographer as well. We initially had a male photographer in our wing, which proved to be very uncomfortable. He kept taking candid shots of our feet...

He clearly thrived from some sort of foot fetish. We called him the "footographer" and casted him across the yard to the men. We invited a woman up to capture Celeste's special day. Then group photos...

My hair and makeup had been done first. I am glowing as if it was my big day. I am so happy. My life has been full of surprises. Baby gives me life and I will be giving him a gift of life really soon. I can't help but look beyond the curtain at him across the yard. The guys are arriving all on time, wearing the gray tuxedos I picked out. Baby is wearing his best man smile. Oh that smile! I have to find my buzzer and get this show on the road. I hope there will be no surprise guests as I have had my share of pop ups, the last one just being a couple months ago . I haven't heard from Jax since. I hope he is doing okay. I must slip into wedding coordinator mode and take my eyes off Baby and my mind off Jax.

"Celeste, I'm going to disappear, if you need anything Fey is here. I'm going to go check on the behind the scenes things."

"Anni wait... I love you! Thank you so much for everything."

"Celeste, everything will be fine and I love you too! See ya in a bit!"

I take a minute to look out across this beautiful field. The day has been kissed goodbye from the sun. Evening is setting in and the color the sky has taken is beautiful! The guests are arriving and I must get across to see Alec before the ceremony starts. He must be all nerves by now. This gravel is eating up my heels as I cross the pathway. I'll call for the crew to direct the cars to park on the smoother pavement. I'll tie this area off with some pretty ribbon and dress it up with a sign and an easel to direct them in the other direction. It will also allow the photographer to get some good shots as they come in down the pathway.

Alec is waiting for me and he looks great. He is very calm.

"Alec, aren't you nervous?

"Sis, I would be more nervous if I couldn't spend my life with her. I'm excited about her finally becoming my wife."

"Gorgeous!" Baby calls out.

"Hi Baby!" I eagerly reply.

"You are stunning. I am one lucky man."

"Yes, my friend you are. My sister is one hell of a woman." Alec interjects.

"Okay, you two save the mushy stuff for the ceremony. I think I need to put some Kleenex in your pockets!" My sarcastic side kicks in.

Baby gives me the biggest kiss and I melt. This man! This has to last forever. I could stare at him for days. The way he rests his fingers in the small of my back makes my world okay. I run back out and he follows me.

"Baby, what is it? Is everything okay?"

"Anacelia, I love you so much. How about we skip this big wedding stuff! Let's get married in an intimate setting, maybe on a roof top with family and friends. We can look down on the city and just embrace the world we live in and have our down time during the vacation."

"Baby, you always read my mind. I would absolutely love that." He kisses me several times and holds on to my fingertips until I am out of his reach."

This man loves me and the look in his eyes at that moment is burned into my brain. I imagine him the entire time I am walking away to gather everyone for group photos before the ceremony!

Ma Ma and Rich look amazing. My little snow princess is ready to toss snow. The bridesmaids are holding their candles and ready to cascade down the pathway, each practicing their poses. I love that there are speakers aligned outside of the building. The soft music playing on the outside is a nice touch... It sets the mood. We set up for fun shots and some more traditional wedding pieces. I'm glad I placed ushers on both sides of these heavy wooden doors for the guests to enter. After everyone is seated I will buzz the bridal party in. The Davenports are here looking like a magazine cover! Rich's closest friends and Celeste's parents have made it as well. The photos of them will be exquisite. They were all responsible for this union. I am grateful. I couldn't have asked for a better sister. This was one arranged relationship that went well. It was amazing to see everyone all in the same place under such great circumstances.

My leg is vibrating! I stashed my cell phone inside of my garter. It's Fey.

"Anni, Celeste is freaking out. Her childhood friend is here. You know the one with the brother!"

"You mean the brother who sexually assaulted her as a child? Is the brother here?"

"No, I don't think so. But she is losing it all the same. It brought up so many memories for her."

"I'll be right there."

I call for my crew to play more processional music as I try to scurry back across with this belly and then call Baby.

"Baby, I need Drei to escort a special set of guests into the ceremony. There is a guest here that is making Celeste nervous. I need Drei on it. Have him find out where the brother is and if he knows about the wedding ASAP! The brother of this girl is the guy that assaulted Celeste as a child. Don't let Alec know what's happening." So much for no surprises...

"You got it, Gorgeous!"

Baby asks Drei to help and he replies, "I got this."

I finally make it across the courtyard. "Celeste, I'm here. What do you need me to do? Do you want her to leave?"

"Anni, I don't want to cause a scene."

"Celeste, this is your day. It's your call." She's sobbing. I need to make a call on this. I make a quick call to Alec.

"Alec! Look up here, where the window is open, for a picture."

"Okay, sis."

"Celeste, look down there. That man is going to be your husband. He will never let anything happen to you. What happened to you is in your past and it will not bleed into your future. Find your peace in him. He is your protector now."

"Anni, you're right. Let's get this ceremony going so I can be in his arms."

"Ok, Fey let's fix her makeup. I'll buzz you when I'm ready for you to bring her down."

"Baby calling" my cell highlights and vibrates.

"Gorgeous, the brother is in jail. She came here with an invited guest. Should we ask her to leave? She is signing the guest book at the moment."

"Have Drei seat her in the Balcony out of Celeste's sight."

"Ok, done!"

Crisis averted. Now back to the entrance where I see Zora and Neale and give them a wink.

I make one last call to the crew and signal the best man and the groom to enter with the officiant. The program should flow after this. The music is perfect. The Bridesmaids play their parts and hit every mark just like rehearsal last night. My little snow princess Kerrigan is making it snow with the help of some snow machines hidden behind some silk fabric on the perimeter of the guest seating. I buzz for the ushers to silently close the doors so that Fey's poem could be heard.

VITA COOP

Love demands a partner to exist

It can be partnered with devotion

It can share the spotlight with loyalty

It has to thrive within comfort, within clarity

These traits are all represented by these two

extraordinary people.

Today, they will join hands in completion and every hour

of their union shall be catered upon by

grace and dedication.

Examination

and

Clarification

Will be worn as an ornament of love at all times

Understanding

Shall ring like a bell's chimes

They were made for each other

Molded and formed to coexist as one

Partnered by the universe

To be tainted by none

Come together guests to witness

This joyous union

Please stand

Buzzer signals, *HEAR COMES THE BRIDE.* The doors are opened and Celeste is standing in a jaw dropping Ivory gown that owns a reflection of a pearl's shimmer. Her bouquet is woven of charcoal silk with strategically placed crystals and hand-picked pearls. The accents partner with her matching belt and head piece. It begins to snow around her. Her train is catching the snow and transporting it down the aisle. The lights were automatically dimmed when the doors were opened. The down lighting is following her down the pathway like a spotlight. Alec is in awe of her. She looks as if she is floating toward him. Her copper toned hair is glowing under the lights and she is literally sparkling. I signal for the doors to close behind her so the lobby can be transformed into the reception area. The ceremony continues and everything is going great. No more surprises. The rows of seating have all been dressed with Kleenex and containers of snow to throw after the pronouncing of, "Man and Wife."

The bridal party begins to leave in a timely but quick manner. The bride and groom follow! I take my container and begin to throw snow so the guests will follow suit. The light weight manufactured snow adorns them as they walk down the aisle. The sight is picture perfect. I will never forget the image. The guests follow into the general area row by row. I'm glad we had the ceremony and the reception at the same venue. Once the doors re-opened the guests were gazing at the transformation outside. My crew is amazing! The Christmas tree was full of gifts underneath that the guests brought in with them. The bar and happy hour stations were set up and the servers were carrying plentiful trays of food while people mingled and gave well wishes to the bride and groom.

It was beautiful outside but now very cold out. The wind was picking up and the ribbon outside was blowing in rhythm. I ran to make sure the videographer captured this. I'll have him wait until this big, black truck moves out of camera's view. GOD has blessed us with a beautiful dusk evening. The sky was painted a beautiful gold and copper with gray clouds. It was a portrait of nature at its best. I was caught in the moment and I felt those fingers resting in the small of my back. My Baby has found me and was holding me while the wind blew his scent right passed me. I'm blessed to be able to look at this man every day of my life. The wind picks up and blows my beautiful copper ribbon away. I grabbed it and my heel got stuck in this awful gravel.

This would be the second moment Baby would save me from a shoe fiasco. I unwillingly stepped out of my shoe just like the night at the café. I realized I was all wrapped up in this ribbon and the gravel had scratched my leg up. But so much blood from scrapes and scratches? What is going on? Everything is fuzzy. I can only see gray and specks of red on this copper ribbon. I can smell and hear fireworks!! But I didn't arrange a fireworks show. Did my family all run out because I stumbled in the gravel? They must be worried about baby Davenport. What is going on? I wondered.

Ma Ma falling to her knees... What's with the fireworks? BABY what's wrong? Get up! Get up! Baby, get up! Rich what's wrong with

Ma Ma? My eyes are so heavy. Somebody please tell me what is going all wrong.

"Baby... Baby..." I call out. He gets up from the crowd. He scans the crowd and he finally sees me. I can only see the image of his gray tuxedo getting closer and closer to me. I can't see him anymore. I can't see anyone. My eyes are heavier.

"She's lost a lot of blood. We have to try to save the baby."

Why does my body hurt so? The light seeping through my eyelid is so bright but still dim at the same time. I can feel it's there, but I can't really see it. I can't tell where I am. I hear voices but unfamiliar. The words, the terminology however is very recognizable.

"Blood pressure's stable."

"Scalpel please."

"Anacelia, please..."

WAIT! That voice, that's my Baby's voice...

"Baby, what's happening?" Am I thinking aloud? Can he hear me?

"Anacelia, if you can hear me please hold on to my voice. Please pull through. I need you." The trembling in his voice is vibrating my soul.

"Baby!" Why can't he hear me?

"Her BP is dropping."

Dear GOD, what is happening? I hear a baby crying. Is this my baby?

"It's a girl!"

GOD, help me! Is this my baby? Could this be my baby girl?

The doctor pleads, "Nurse, take the baby. Dad, please follow the nurse."

"Doctor, I don't know what to do. Is my baby girl okay?" Baby asks.

"Is Anni ok?" Baby continues with his tear filled questions.

I can feel him turn toward me. He asks me, "Anni are you ok? Anni are you ok?"

This phrase no longer triggers laughter. I'M NOT OK!

The doctor speaks again. "Mr. Davenport, the nurse will lead you outside."

I realize I'm under. No one can hear me. During a C-section, I'm supposed to be conscious, but I'm blocked. Why am I blocked? Why am I under? The father is always allowed in the operating room during the procedure. If it's a routine procedure, why am I under? Why are they asking Baby to leave? I should be able to talk and to see my baby. Something else is wrong. My vision is opaque. I can't see. The voices fade away again. Baby... Ba....

"We're losing her!"

"Father GOD, my choices in life have been questionable but I ask you to save my family. It should have been me that was shot. PLEASE SAVE MY ANNI! Spare my new daughter, Anniston, A name deriving from her beautiful mother. I will honor her wishes and keep the name..."

"Mr. Davenport, would you like to hold your daughter?" The nurse interrupts his prayer.

"Yes, very much..." Baby replies and tears are dropping into Anniston's big blue eyes.

"GOD, she has my eyes. This pain is none I have ever felt. This beautiful child in my arms could be my end and my beginning!" Baby exclaims in mercy.

"Mr. Davenport..."

"Yes, Doctor. I've been waiting for hours. Our family is waiting in the lobby. How is she?"

He reports. "We did everything we could. She slipped into a coma. She was shot twice. One blow to her leg but the second grazed the base of her head. We removed the bullet but we could not save her sight. Anni is now blind."

Standing there in a blood drenched tuxedo, holding his new baby girl, he vociferously realizes, "She will never see our baby's eyes are like mine."

CPSIA information can be obtained
at www.ICGtesting.com
Printed in the USA
FSOW01n0114301116
27906FS